Jane F

From Now On

This is a work of fiction. Names, characters,
business organizations and products,
places and incidents either are the product of the author's
imagination or are used fictitiously, and any resemblance
to any actual persons, living or dead, events,
or locales is entirely coincidental.

Copyright © Jane Francis 2001

The moral right of the author has been asserted.

All rights reserved. No part of this book may be reproduced
or transmitted in any form or by any means, electronic
or mechanical, including photocopying, recording,
or by any information storage and retrieval system,
without permission in writing from the copyright owner.

Condition of Sale
This book is sold subject to the condition that it shall not,
by way of trade or otherwise, be lent, re-sold,
hired out or otherwise circulated without the publisher's
prior consent in any form of binding or cover other than
that in which it is published and without a similar condition
including this condition being imposed on the subsequent purchaser.

First printed in New Zealand by
Amazing. But true Ltd, PO Box 207, Orewa 1461, NZ.
http://www.jane-francis.com

Printed and bound in New Zealand

ISBN 0-473-07973-9

For

Peter, Pernelle, Mitchell, Calvin and Brittany

with love

Part One

- 1 -

She was in labor when the thought first came to her - if one of these babies were a boy she would find a way to switch him for another. And what would she do if she had two boys? Nothing, she decided, nothing at all.

It was 7.33 p.m. 24 December 1977, and seventeen-year-old Katrina Dudek had been in the delivery suite eleven hours when the doctor told her of his decision to intervene. He left the room soon to reappear carrying a pair of stainless steel forceps and wearing green rubber boots and a white plastic apron over his clothes.

Katrina squeezed her eyes shut, feeling the blunt thrust of something force its way inside her. Moments later she involuntarily opened her eyes to see the doctor pull, arms shaking and face reddening, on the handles of the tongs that were now wedged internally. Disregarding the screams of the mother he tugged with as much strength as he might have used to pull a car from a ditch until with one final grunt, the baby's head was released from the birth canal.

Katrina sank back against a pile of pillows and closed her eyes, her head filled with a noise that echoed like shock waves in a stone quarry.

The nurse took the baby from the doctor and lifted her into Katrina's line of vision. 'Blue eyes and blonde hair, she's going to be beautiful, just like you,' she said.

But Katrina kept her eyes shut; she didn't open them to watch the doctor cut and knot the umbilical cord, nor did she see her baby take her first innocent squint at the world.

At the back of the delivery suite a nurse sponge-cleaned the baby before wrapping her in a blanket and handing her to a colleague to take from the room.

The doctor waited at the foot of the bed seemingly oblivious to a streak of blood smeared diagonally across the front of his apron, his latex-gloved hands poised awkwardly in the air.

Soon enough, Katrina felt another contraction and let out a low groan and whimpered. Overcome by an incredible bearing-down sensation she lifted her upper body and pushed with all the power of nature until finally the baby's head broke through. Exhausted, she dropped back against the pillows; the relief, now it was over, felt almost too much to bear.

'It's a boy,' said the nurse. 'A boy and a girl - aren't you lucky!'
Lucky?
Katrina lay motionless, drained, and defeated. Just what sort of life might she have given that small boy? In a remote part of her brain she heard a baby cry, a woman's voice and some crooning, and the squeaking wheels of a trolley, the clang of surgical instruments and rip of disposable packaging. She winced, and then cried softly with her hands over her face as the doctor stitched her perineum. With a final snip of the scissors, she felt the warmth of a blanket as it was laid over her. It was only when she believed she was on her own that she opened her eyes and was surprised to see a nurse still standing beside her.

'I'm not keeping them,' Katrina said.

- 2 -

Eight and a half months earlier, babies didn't feature in Katrina's life plans.

It was the middle of April and Katrina woke to sun shining through the lattice windows, and squinted at the light that reflected off a glossy Count Dracula poster pinned to the wall. In large, untidy handwriting, scribbled on a raggedy-edged banner, the words *Hemophilia Sucks,* was attached below. Katrina rolled over, wanting to sleep again, but then she remembered last night and the vampire smiled lustily, his victim draped, long black hair trailing, tragically in his arms.

'Katrina, get up, you'll be late for school,' her father shouted up the stairs.

'C-o-m-ing,' she yelled back, lethargically.

She dragged herself out of bed, giving the Count a long hard stare. How she'd love to rip his self-satisfied leer off the wall but she didn't want to risk hurting her twin brother's feelings. David already had enough to cope with living with hemophilia, a bleeding disorder that affects mainly males.

Going to the mirror, she lifted her blonde hair to check her neck for any signs of last night's petting. She dressed quickly then went to join her father for breakfast.

'David and Mom gone to the hospital?' she asked.

'As usual,' he scowled.

Katrina poured some cereal into a plate. 'You could at least take turns every now and again,' she said, blaming the nights her mother spent with David getting his treatment from the hospital for making her mother look older than her forty-three years.

'Someone's got to earn a living round here,' he grunted.

Katrina sat at the farthest seat, trying to block the sounds of his lips smacking and teeth grinding as he shoveled in his cereal.

'It's Mom's birthday on Wednesday,' she said. 'Have you thought what you'd get her?'

Taking a final slurp, he clanged his spoon down and stood up, walking away, leaving his plate at the table without giving a second thought to tidying up.

'I'm getting her a women's lib book,' Katrina said, 'it's about time she burnt her bra.'

He turned to look at her, his hand combing a solitary few long hairs over his balding pate. 'I got her something,' he said, sullenly, checking his reflection in a mirror beside the fridge. 'Don't forget Bob's coming round tonight. Shelley and the kids aren't back for another couple of weeks,' he mumbled, before heading towards the back door and slamming it on his way out.

Katrina tidied the kitchen then made her lunch and went upstairs to pack some books into her school bag. Pulling a face at Count Dracula, she thought about David and how unfair life seemed to him. To his way of thinking she'd inherited the brains, good looks, perfect health and now, in the last six months since her interest in Scott had blossomed, she'd unintentionally stolen his best friend's affections too.

Drawing a deep breath, Katrina picked up her school bag, trying to unleash the suffocating despair and guilt that throbbed in the background like a phantom amputee limb, always present yet never there. She locked the house and walked to the end of the driveway where Scott waited by the wrought iron gate with his back to her, a towel tucked under one arm, his long wavy hair curled into ringlets, dripping a wet patch on his shoulders.

'Hi,' she called out, trying to sound casual. 'So you made it to the pool?'

Turning, he smiled shyly. 'Yeah.' After all the beer he'd drunk at last night's party, she was surprised he'd felt like training. She looked down the tree-lined street and waited for a bus to pass, then kissed him quickly on the cheek, laughing teasingly when he recoiled, embarrassed that someone might have seen.

'Isn't David coming?' he asked.

'No,' she said, and started walking. 'I was asleep when Mom took him to hospital early this morning.'

'It must've been when he banged into that trestle,' Scott said.

Katrina nodded. Scott had been a friend of the twins since they were toddlers; they were so close he'd learnt to anticipate David's injuries like a brother.

'He must have hit his elbow harder than he let on,' she agreed.

'Do you think he enjoyed the party?' Scott asked.

Katrina shrugged. She doubted it. Lately David had missed so much school he didn't stand a hope of getting a scholarship; he'd probably end up repeating the year while all his friends left home to develop their exciting new careers. Was it really any wonder he was so depressed, that he'd told her he'd felt like ending it all?

Nearing the school, the road became busier with cars and motorbikes dropping people off. Scott dodged a low-hanging tree branch that grew over the sidewalk. Stepping into Katrina's path, his arm knocked hers, 'Sorry,' he said.

'That's okay,' she said, then added, 'I had fun last night.'

'Me too,' he said.

Katrina saw a group of friends up ahead. She reached out and stopped Scott, there was something else she wanted to make clear. 'But I don't think we should tell him, do you?'

Scott shook his head, and his soft brown eyes smiled and she knew then that last night was nice, it'd been special, but for everyone's sake, it wasn't to be anything more that.

'It's hard to believe this is my last day,' he said, 'I'm going to miss you, you know.'

'I'll miss you too,' she said quietly, knowing Scott and his family were shifting to Oregon this weekend and that though she swore she'd write and keep in touch, deep down it was inevitable they would drift apart. She turned and headed towards her classroom, preoccupied with grief, not thinking until later that morning, what if she was now pregnant?

At first the idea entered her mind like an item that needed to be added to a shopping list, then it morphed into an ominous feeling of dread that forced her to visit the library at lunchtime. Hiding in the human biology aisle with pink diagrams of ovaries and fallopian tubes, she tried to calculate her risk of pregnancy, closing the book or turning the page each time someone drew near.

In the afternoon it became even harder to control the panic that infested her mind, and she was glad when the school bell rang and she was able to hurry home.

Now as she stood at the kitchen sink peeling the potatoes, she felt like throwing up with worry. A baby would ruin everything. Both she and Scott had such grand ambitions for their careers. Scott wanted to become a lawyer and Katrina was going to make a name in medicine. All her life she'd promised David that with her high grades in science, she'd find a way to prevent others from having to suffer a half-life like his.

She cut the potatoes into pieces, and washed the carrots and beans, savagely dicing and scraping them into the pot. Now reality had her in its grip it seemed ludicrous that they'd taken such a risk - yet in the heat of last night's passion it'd seemed so right. 'I know I'm leaving,' Scott had said, whispering in her ear, pressing his body against hers in the cramped confines of the backyard tree-hut, 'but I really want you to be my first lover.' The offer of losing their innocence together had seemed so irresistible, accentuated by the knowledge it was to be their last night together until heaven-only-knows when. 'Please, Katrina, even if it's only the once - it will still be forever - and that's something that can never be undone.'

Katrina added a pinch of salt to the water and banged the saucepan lid down. If the worse came to the worst, she'd have to find out how to get an abortion she supposed. Hearing the sound of an engine, she looked out the window to see Bob drive in and park his brand new Chrysler. Sun glinted off its shiny new wheel caps, a flamboyant reminder of his recent big win at the races.

'Hi ya babe,' Bob called out, the flares on his denims flapping as he sauntered in.

'Hi,' she replied, trying to sound casual, desperately hoping she wouldn't blush under his gaze. Removing the vegetable peelings from the sink, she felt his eyes roam her body and thought she'd die of embarrassment if he knew how attracted she was to him. In his early thirties, dark eyed and bearded with a slightly martyred look, he had a way about him that made her feel grown up, sexy.

Bob worked alongside her father as an accountant at a hardware wholesaler in town and over their evening meal they gossiped about people at work, and Bob's wife who'd gone home to visit her parents in Holland for a time.

After they'd eaten, the two men retired to the living room. David went to bed and Katrina helped their mother clear the mess away. Through the wall, they could hear the occasional clink and fizz of the gin and tonic bottles, and loud roars of laughter.

Katrina nodded to the noise next door. 'He always has all the fun, why do you put up with that?'

'What choice do I have?' her mother said, twisting a towel inside a wineglass.

'You could leave,' Katrina said.

'And what would I live on? I'm not qualified for anything, and besides, who'd look after David?'

Katrina scrubbed the last saucepan, hating the way her mother so readily played the martyr and victim role. There was no way, Katrina vowed, she would ever let any man control *her* destiny.

They finished the dishes then pulled up chairs and chatted around the table for a while. The night darkened outside.

'It's time you went to bed,' Katrina said, noticing how tired her mother looked with black rings under her eyes.

'Can we have some coffee in here,' her father yelled through the wall.

Katrina put her hands firmly on her mother's thin shoulders and ushered her towards her bedroom, up the stairs. 'You go, I'll get it,' Katrina said.

The water had just boiled when Bob came into the kitchen,

clumsily sneaking up behind her and touching her bottom.

'Don't!' Katrina turned and slapped him, though not quite as hard as she'd like.

'Hey, chill out,' he slurred, his eyes appraising her, smoke curling from the marijuana joint he held between his fingers. 'Try some,' he said, holding the roll-your-own close to her face.

Annoyed, Katrina snatched it from him, then had a rebellious thought. She took the small fag from him and met his gaze. Inhaling slowly, she coughed with her mouth closed and fought the smoke down her gullet before passing the roach back.

Her father entered the room. 'Forget the coffee, I'm going to bed.' He stumbled forwards, crashing into Bob. 'Hey man, you're stoned,' he said, collapsing against the nearest wall in laughter, a drunken hiss.

Eventually he collected himself together. 'Ya wanna crash here?' Then turning to Katrina, he asked, 'Where're the blankets kept?'

Katrina gave him a 'how could you not know look?' and then because she knew he'd wake the whole house trying to find the cupboard they were stored in, she went to get some blankets, passing her father climbing the stairs on his way to bed.

When she returned to the lounge, the lights were off, only two small red and green lights on the record player glowed in the dark.

'Here y'are,' Katrina said, throwing the blankets in Bob's general direction.

'Is that any way to treat your guest?' Bob asked, patting the cushion on the floor beside him. 'Come and sit beside me, you've gotta learn how to chill out.'

Katrina hesitated. After all she'd read in the women's magazines lately about sexual liberation - owning your body, men the oppressors, girls can do anything - it felt like a challenge.

'Come on-n-n,' he said, rolling some leaves into a cigarette paper, licking the edge, making a tight roll. 'Put some music on,' he pleaded, 'how about some Pink Floyd?'

Stepping over him, Katrina lifted the lid of the turntable, placed the stylus on the edge of the vinyl groove, and waited for the music to begin.

Bob held out the cigarette and she took it, then flopped on a cushion beside him. 'That's it, now you tell me everything,' he said, placing the joint between her lips, his hand shaking as he lit the match.

Boldly holding his gaze, Katrina inhaled then lifted her chin, pursed her lips, and blew a steady stream of gray smoke into the air. Bob moved closer, kissed her neck and placed one hand on a breast, gently rolling the nipple between his fingers with obvious desire. Resisting the urge to pull back, Katrina dared herself to go through with this; if he was fool enough to play this game with her, she would make sure he paid.

It was Christmas Day 1977, and the Christmas tree on the ward was covered in white sequined booties and sparkling blue-glass balls. The angel on top had golden wings and a halo that flashed with twinkling lights; it held an open songbook and continuously sang 'Hark the Herald Angels Sing' in a high-pitched electronic chime that seemed to go a pitch higher each time it was repeated.

A nurse walked past the tree and looked up. 'Oh, for God's sake *shut up.*'

She opened the door to Room 14 and entered, giving her patient a cheery smile. 'Did Santa bring you anything nice?'

Katrina gave her a wistful look. 'You don't get anything if you've been a bad girl.'

'I'm sure you can't have done anything that bad.'

'That's what *you* think,' Katrina said, turning her head and taking a deep breath. It felt wonderful now the babies weren't inside, pushing her lungs up.

Since her arrival in the ward last night Katrina had been surprised how weak she was, mentally and physically. Everything about having the twins had been far worse than she'd ever imagined: the tiredness, back pain, sleeplessness, constipation. Even in the first month of pregnancy she'd experienced an all-pervasive sickness that would last all day, sometimes making her vomit. After the fifteenth week the nausea had been replaced with acid-burning indigestion as the two babies fought her intestines for space within her. Powerless to control them, she'd hated the way they kicked and punched the walls of her bowel, kidney, heart and lungs like terrorists who had hijacked her body with no regard for what condition they would leave her in.

The nurse checked her patient's temperature and blood pressure, the position of her womb and the condition of her stitches. Writing up the medical notes, she told Katrina what she needed to know about post-natal depression, and stomach and pelvic floor exercises.

'I know you're young dear, but trust me, you do need to do those exercises, especially with twins, you've got twice the reason.' The nurse started to make the bed, pulling the sheets tight under Katrina's feet before smoothing the blankets and arranging the pillows. A hint of perfume, possibly baby talcum powder, wafted in the air. 'Were there twins in your family?'

'I'm a twin, well, I was,' Katrina said, her voice trembling; it still hurt to talk about David in the past tense. The nurse stopped what was she doing; Katrina was used to people not knowing how to respond. First they would avoid looking at her then they would find something to do, and a reason to leave the room.

'Things like that can take a long time,' said the nurse, suddenly making a big deal of tucking in a corner of the blanket. 'Would you like me to get you some icepacks for the swelling around your stitches?'

'Yes, please.'

'How about some painkillers?'

'That'd be good.'

'I'll get you some.'

'Thanks.'

The nurse left and Katrina rolled onto her stomach, the weight of several spare folds of skin flopping loosely as she turned - but what joy! The simple pleasure of lying on her stomach was hers once more.

As promised, the nurse returned with the icepacks and helped Katrina gingerly position herself on top, the movement and then the biting cold making her cry out in pain until the numbness seeped through.

Lying back, she tried to sleep but could not. Soon she'd be free to do whatever she liked, thanks to Bob and his money. 'Shit!' had been his first word when she told him the news; then he'd muttered something about God, insisting he make some arrangements for her to have the babies where nobody would know. 'And of course, I'll see you right,' he'd said. 'You mustn't ruin your career prospects, not over some silly mistake like this.' Katrina sniffed, even now the words 'silly mistake' jarred painfully, for only she knew she hadn't made just one mistake, but several. And in reality it was hard to dismiss two live babies under the heading 'mistake'; just what sort of reason is that for being born?

Taking a tissue from her bedside locker, Katrina wiped the tears from her face. Two hundred thousand dollars was an excellent return on effort, she thought grimly - if only the dark feelings would go away.

Katrina pressed the buzzer for a nurse to help her to the bathroom, her legs feeling too shaky for her to walk on her own. Partway down the corridor Katrina and the nurse flattened themselves against the Christmas tree to allow a bed to be wheeled past. Serenaded by the singing angel, they stepped back into the middle of the passageway. Moments later, Katrina felt a tug at her hair and turned, thrusting her hand out, she caught the tree as it veered towards her. The angel fell to the floor and bounced, and suddenly the ward sounded unnaturally quiet.

'Damn! I think I've broken it,' Katrina said, looking helpless with the tree's branches bristling around her.

The door of the room opposite opened and out shuffled a patient. The name-card on the door read: *Roseanne Bryant, mother of Adam*. Glimpsing Katrina under the tree, Roseanne had a brief moment of incomprehension before she burst out laughing. As if on cue, the angel resumed its chiming. Surprised and relieved, Katrina and the nurse started to giggle then the three of them began to reassemble the tree.

It was late at night when Katrina went to the nursery. All visitors had been sent home and the lights were off in the rooms, with only a few night-lights left on in the corridor.

Katrina stood beside the clear perspex, double bassinet and when she saw her little boy stir she gently unfolded him from the cocoon of blankets and lifted him from his bed. She was relieved the movement didn't waken her pink-bonneted baby girl who was snoring rhythmically, some mucus rattling in her nasal passages.

Holding the boy close to her chest, she watched him yawn, scrunch his face and whimper before turning toward her breasts in the forlorn hope of finding a comforting nipple to latch onto.

She offered him her little finger and he sucked fiercely on the tip of it while she carried him to a diaper-changing table at the other end of the room. Lying him down, she looked over at another fair skinned, blonde-haired baby sleeping in a bassinet positioned under an ultraviolet heat-lamp. The nametag was circled in blue. *Sex: Male. Born: 6.30 p.m., 24 December 1977. Name: Adam. Baby of Mr and Mrs Bryant.*

With her ears pricked, Katrina quickly wriggled the hospital identity bracelet from her baby's wrist before slipping it into a pocket of her nightgown. The corridor was quiet except for the murmur of the night nurses scheduling duty rosters at their station.

Adam stirred and let out a couple of half-hearted cries. Reaching over she rocked his bassinet, shushing him to be quiet, but his cries intensified. At the sound of footsteps, she pulled her hand away and made a display of attending to her own baby.

A nurse appeared at the door. 'Are you all right in there?'

Katrina nodded, her heart thumping furiously. 'He's dirty, I'm changing him,' she replied.

The nurse moved in beside Adam's bassinet and felt his brow then lifted the heat-lamp away. She took the clipboard from the end of his small cot and made some notes on Adam's medical charts before tiptoeing out of the room, her footsteps receding down the corridor.

Alone again, Katrina reached for Adam's hand to quickly swap the identity bracelets.

In a hurry now, she whisked Adam from his bed and rolled her baby into his place roughly tucking the blankets around him as he started to cry. Knowing she could only have a moment to spare, she picked Adam up and held him against her shoulder and made soothing, crooning noises to allay the suspicions of the nurse who would no doubt reappear. Now the swap was done, Katrina wondered if anyone would ever know, or if they would ever care.

- 4 -

Katrina had no difficulty finding the red-brick social services building that sat like an outpost at the back of the hospital grounds. The grass felt cool underfoot and the breeze was fresh against her face - a welcome contrast to the cloying hormone-infused air of the maternity ward.

Arriving early, she stopped and picked some daisies, folding the stalks around their heads, pulling the stems back, jettisoning them into the distance.

At five minutes to ten she opened the door and stepped inside, cautiously, taken aback at first by the eerie stillness of the room, its atmosphere: dank and dingy, reeking of vacuous indecision. Katrina had a choice of three chipped, wooden seats with stress fractures around the rivets or a low-legged purple vinyl sofa whose cushions were cracked in fine beige lines like a palmist's hand. She chose the sofa and, knowing no one was looking, dropped her bottom loudly into it. *Splat!*

The seat felt cold and hard and dirty. *Yuk!* Her legs sweated against the vinyl; her fingers picked at the well-worn purple edging on the armrest. Some tired magazines spilled off a small table, Katrina took one and settled back, flicking through the pages with its promises of scandal and gratuitous titillation that felt as relevant under the circumstances as a box of matches at a forest fire. Snapping the glossy paper between her fingers in a continuous page-turning medley, she glanced at the pictures and headlines. Full of lies and trivia, she thought, a typical woman's magazine.

At the sound of footsteps on the concrete path outside, Katrina put the magazine back on the table. The door banged open and in flounced a woman, mid-forties, a hospital badge pinned to her gaudy turquoise and orange tie-dyed dress. Wafting a cocktail of herbal soaps and shampoos, she motioned to Katrina to follow her down the mottled green linoleum passageway to a private interview room.

Katrina took a seat and waited for the woman to stop rifling through her pile of papers. After what seemed like an eternity she finally said, 'Please just call me Maggie,' giving Katrina a squinty smile that looked as if it had been lifted from page three of the social workers' manual.

Katrina sat through the woman's spiel. Speeches one to four: This must be a difficult time for you; You'll look back on this one day and know you did the right thing; We will give you our full support; Don't worry, the children will be well looked after.

Although Maggie had never given a child up for adoption she felt a bond 'woman-to-woman' she said, continuing to ooze essence of third world into the increasing heat of the room.

Maggie covered all the legal issues, touched on women's rights, privacy, open adoptions, and what might happen when the children were old enough to search for their mother. On and on.

Katrina despised the assumptions Maggie was making - that one day she'd meet a nice man and want to settle down. *Don't you realise, you stupid bitch, I don't want to be a mother. I don't want to join that sorority.* She'd seen how babies made a mockery of women as they turned them into mothers. The ward was full of leaking breast milk, sore nipples, fat ankles, hysterical high-pitched voices - a cacophony of complaining women, suffering again. Motherhood as institutionalised martyrdom; she knew that was something Maggie would never understand.

The minutes ticked by and Maggie continued her lecture, her mouth moving in segments like the jaws of a stick insect - perhaps one from the Congo, one that lived on the husks of an exotic plant they used to make essential oils. *For God's sake, let's get on with it. Let me be free!*

Maggie stopped talking and twitched her head from side to side.

'Are you all right? Is there something you wanted to say?' She knitted her brow, giving Katrina the sort of look that Katrina supposed was designed to get her to open up, to reveal all her inner emotions.

'Can't we just sign the papers? I mean, what are we waiting for?'

Maggie blinked, then resumed the speech about how she wanted to be sure that Katrina wouldn't have any regrets later on but Katrina interrupted her. 'I know all that, can't we just get to the point?'

'Do you have anyone who can support you through this, friends or family?'

'I … don't … need … anybody,' Katrina said coldly. She'd got into this mess on her own, and now she'd deceived her parents into thinking she was at university already, she was completely on her own.

Somewhere outside a lawnmower started up, the noise seemed to hum and bounce around the walls behind them.

Maggie persisted, 'Legally, I must ask you to sign this form. It states that you, Katrina Dudek, release the twins to the State who will assume responsibility for finding them a kind and loving family who will raise the children as their own. If you would like access, or photographs, or progress reports on the children's welfare, the parents I have selected would be happy to oblige although I did tell them you weren't interested. Do you still feel that way?'

'Yes.'

'All right, that just about covers it. Is there anything you would like me to tell them?'

'No. Are we done yet?'

'Nearly. There is one last issue, covered under this clause here.' Maggie pointed to some small print at the bottom of the page. 'It specifies your wish that the twins remain together. It isn't compulsory you sign this, but we recommend you do so for the sake of the children, in the event of the adoptive parents dying.'

Katrina didn't appear to have heard. She was thinking about David, pushing away the guilt, glad he wasn't alive to know what she was doing.

'Yeah, all right. I'll sign it,' she said.

'And there's another box you might like to tick…'

Katrina read the item then ticked the box. Her request that she not be contacted later in life was now official, although there was nothing to legally prevent the children from contacting her - if they could find her that is.

'Do you want to have one last look? Once you've signed these papers you'll have officially given all legal rights over to the babies' new parents.'

Without answering or even bothering to look up, Katrina pulled the clipboard to her side of the table and scrawled an enormous signature across the bottom of the page.

'Some people feel the emotion later, sometimes years after. Here, take my card,' Maggie said, 'and if you ever feel the need to talk to somebody please give me a call.'

Katrina refused the card. Instead she stood abruptly, her chair screeching loudly on the linoleum.

Maggie put the card back in her bag. 'I'll leave you a brochure.'

An indefatigable optimist - or just plain stupid, Katrina didn't know which - Maggie placed the brochure on the table. 'How do you feel?' she asked.

'Great!' said Katrina. 'I've already forgotten I had them.'

The outer door closed with a jolt. For a moment or two Katrina stood on the doorstep, her eyes adjusting to the glare, enjoying the sun's rays warming her face. No longer in a rush, she wandered around the hospital grounds before returning to the ward.

When she got back to her room she found a nurse looking through her medical charts. She looked up and smiled warmly at Katrina. 'One last check-up, my dear, and you can be on your way.' She handed Katrina a thermometer, and as she did so she asked softly, 'Are you going to be all right?'

Katrina held the thermometer firmly under her tongue and nodded. This was nobody's business but her own.

Once the check-up was over Katrina collected her clothes, and the cosmetics she had put in the bedside locker. 'Here, you dropped something,' said the nurse, holding out a metal flower. 'Wait a minute, there must be another piece somewhere, this looks like it's broken.'

'No, no, that's the way it's meant to be.' Katrina said accepting the small metal token. The flower was part of a love-me, love-me-not daisy clock that Scott had been making for her. They'd seen one in a design store while shopping last year and Scott had promised that if he made one daisy each month, even allowing for interruptions, he'd easily have completed the clock in time for Christmas this year.

January's daisy was at the one o'clock position and had eleven petals - she loves me. February's daisy had ten petals - she loves me not. March had nine - she loves me. April was when she'd made love to him, and then he'd left and though he'd written once, and she'd seen him for the last time at David's funeral, he must have forgotten all about the clock.

Katrina placed the daisy on top of her clothes and noisily closed the zip. At the funeral she'd worn clothes to disguise her four-month pregnancy, and was certain neither Scott nor any of her family would have guessed. She'd wanted to tell him about the pregnancy but she knew she could not - the babies might not have been his, and how then would she have explained the money?

She picked up her bags and walked past the nurses' station, waving through the open door to Adam's mother who called out, 'Mind the tree!' Katrina grinned back. In the next moment she passed the long narrow nursery window and caught sight of the back of the familiar turquoise and orange tie-dyed dress. Opposite Maggie a man in a red-checked shirt held a baby. Beside him stood a tall, wavy-haired woman with a large roman nose, and theatrically-arched, plucked eyebrows, who lifted a small blanketed parcel to her face, her lips pursed in readiness to kiss the small baby's cheek. Perhaps the movement of Katrina passing by had caught the woman's attention making her look up and over the baby, but for one unforgettable fraction of eternity their eyes met before Katrina hastily averted her gaze. Determined she would have no regrets, her stride didn't falter as she stepped on past the window, down the corridor, and out into the impossibly bright sunshine to the rest of her life.

Part Two

- 5 -

Twenty-three years later

At the end of a shell pathway that weaved among flowering flax bushes and palms, the flaps of a white marquee gently billowed in a light breeze. On either side of its entrance, two topiaries shaped like doves shimmered with a luscious plumage of white sequins and pearls. Stereo speakers hidden in the garden played the mellow tones of a Barry White serenade.

Inside the marquee, a young man and his mother waited, a dozen pink heart-shaped balloons floating above their heads. Across the aisle from them were two empty chairs and in front was a cane table on which was placed a crystal bowl of water with frangipani flowers floating on top. Sunlight passed through the crystal, the rays separating into myriads of tiny rainbow shards of brilliant purples, greens and reds which flickered across the open pages of the gold-edged wedding register that lay to one side.

Dressed in tight suede pants with a silver-studded belt, buckled boots and a black polo top, the young man stood up and raised his hand to hit a balloon. Watching it bump into the others, causing a ruckus overhead, he smiled gleefully. 'A romantic fool, I'll say that about Gemini,' he said, sitting down again.

Pamela clicked her tongue in disapproval. Everything about her son's appearance and mannerisms advertised his sexuality and availability. She wished he would sit still, he'd always had energy to burn. 'You two couldn't be more different if you tried,' she said, the emotion of the wedding triggering a memory of the first time she'd met the twins. How she'd held them against her heart, admiring their perfect faces, wondering like any new mother - and perhaps because she wasn't the birth mother, even more so - what the future may hold.

Hudson smirked and moved towards his mother to give her a playful peck on the cheek. Instinctively Pamela blocked him by putting her shoulder up and turning her head away, not wanting his lips to smudge the chalky layer of foundation that covered her face.

'I knew you'd love the nose stud,' Hudson said. 'It's a half-carat, you know.'

Pamela gave him a thin smile and responded in the way she knew he'd expect. 'I don't know Hudson,' she said. 'Couldn't you have left it out just this once? Sometimes I can't help wishing you were a little more conventional.'

'You mean a little less San Franciscan and a bit more Texan,' he said, giving her a cheeky grin.

Pamela let out a half-hearted laugh, an insincere attempt to shrug off her prejudice against her son's flamboyant homosexuality. 'Something like that,' she said, wondering if she'd made him like that, or was it predestined?

Hudson lifted his arm as if he were going to give her a hug but something caught her attention. She grabbed his hand. 'What are all those bruises?'

'They're not bruises, they're love bites.'

'I should've known,' she said, dropping his hand abruptly. Surely if he'd been her real son, he wouldn't have been quite this ostentatious?

Hudson grinned, then swiveled his head to look over his shoulder. 'Here they come,' he said.

Pamela smiled, the lines around her eyes crumpling into the hard-won folds of the social mask she'd worn for the past fifty-one years. Straightening her back, she tried to pull her stomach in as she turned to face the mother of the groom, reminded once again that even if she did lose twenty kilograms she'd still never look that good.

Oh, my God, she can even get away with leopard print! Pamela forced her smile wider, feeling the ache in her cheeks; they would soon be bonded as mothers-in-law, yet if it weren't for their children they would have nothing in common.

She knew Barbara's story: Only one child, Clint, to her first husband, an Olympic sprint athlete who failed to make the finals and later developed a problem with alcohol and gambling. Clint was thirteen when she filed for divorce, and the father had never been seen or heard of since. Now Barbara was happily remarried to a property-developer millionaire.

Barbara and Steve took their seats, and Pamela cynically wondered what she had done to attract Barbara into her life. At the sound of footsteps behind them the small group turned to look at the approaching bridal couple, and Pamela let out a short gasp, her daughter looking like a Greek goddess statue from an eighteenth century garden, soft and ethereal, not a bit like her.

With one hand the bride carried a small bouquet of flowers in muted shades of cream, pastel yellows and pale pistachio green, the other holding the groom's hand. He looked the ideal partner: tanned, square-jawed, white-teethed and athletic looking, every inch his mother's son.

A man wearing a purple velvet waistcoat and long blonde-hair pulled into a pony-tail, lagged behind the bridal party, taking a narrow, less noticeable path to the left, reappearing a moment later behind the table at the front of the marquee. The marriage celebrant organised his notes on the table, and when he was ready beckoned to the bride and groom to take their places in front of him. A professional crowd pleaser, he motioned for silence before theatrically raising his ring-studded hands to 'humbly give thanks to the Lord'.

'Friends,' he said, 'we are gathered here today to celebrate the glorious union of Clint and Gemini as they take their sacred wedding vows. In an earlier chat with Clint and Gemini they told me they didn't want a long speech or sermon, or even poems. They told me love is a feeling in their hearts - and no words can describe its strength. So without further ado it is my pleasure to invite you all to witness their special vows.'

Turning to Clint, he asked: 'Clint James Harrison, do you take Gemini Jasmine Crawford to be your lawfully wedded wife?'

'I do.'

'Do you promise to love her for better or worse, richer or poorer, in sickness and in health, to have and to hold from this day forward, till death do you part?'

'I do.'

The celebrant led Gemini through the same vows then asked Clint for the rings. Clint slid the ring over Gemini's finger, repeating his words after the celebrant. He turned to the wedding party, saying, 'Sometimes I think I must be the luckiest man alive then I wonder if it's really true. Have I actually died and gone to heaven?'

Gemini turned Clint's face to hers, and said in a soft voice but one that everyone could hear, 'I love you too. When are you meant to kiss the bride?'

That evening Gemini trawled her fingers though the spa bath bubbles. 'It was perfect,' she said. 'The wedding was everything I'd ever wanted. No fuss, no pretension. Just us and the people who really matter.' Clint sat beside her, one hand resting on her thigh. Again he felt a familiar tingling in his groin; stroking her thigh, he edged his hand upwards and leant forwards to kiss her.

'You're insatiable!' Gemini said, catching hold of his hand, pulling him closer to her, sinking into the warm bubbles.

Later that night they walked on the beach. The surf that had crashed all day had died to gentle ripples that now rolled in whispers across the crushed shells. A crescent moon shed light on the wavy line of footsteps the lovers left as they shared ideas, their conversation moving them together at times, then apart.

After a while they stopped and Gemini curled her toes into the sand, dislodging some of the larger shells in order to admire their shapes. She picked a few up and twirled them in her hand, their curves catching a pearly sheen in the moonlight. 'Aren't they beautiful?' she sighed. 'I'm going to take them home and make something to remind me of these moments forever.'

Clint smiled and tapped the pockets of his jeans. He stopped when he'd found what he was looking for, and put his hand in and pulled out a small square box. 'Close your eyes and open your hands,' he said, placing the box into Gemini's open palms, watching her feel the sides of the box until she found the tiny clasp and unclipped it. She lifted the lid, and when he said she could, opened her eyes to see a gold scallop-shell locket attached to a fine gold chain.

'Oh, Clint, it's gorgeous,' she said, giving him a quick hug then taking the necklace from its box. 'I hope you've engraved something special on the inside.'

She eased her fingernails into the parting on the side and opened the locket, turning it to catch the moonlight, she read the inscription: *Gem. Love you - now and forever. Clint.*

Reaching out and pulling him towards her, she kissed him hungrily, trailing her hand down his back, she playfully caressed his buttocks until her fingers found their way around to the zip on the front of his jeans. 'I want you to make love to me in a way we'll remember for always,' she said tenderly.

They hastily discarded their clothing and made a crumpled bed, their hips moving in unison to the whisper of waves shuffling shells on the beach. Clint thrust slowly and deeply until they reached the height of their excitement and Gemini lovingly met his gaze - for this time they both knew they were making more than love, this time they were trying to make a baby.

- 6 -

Clint was nearly at his office when his mobile phone rang. After the honeymoon, he found work seemed even more boring than usual. He answered the call, then turned the car around and headed back home, phoning his secretary to cancel his appointments that day.

Then he pressed speed dial. 'Gem, guess what?' he said, not pausing for a response. 'They've called me back later today for a final interview!'

'That's wonderful,' Gemini replied, her voice sounded flat and distracted. 'I can't talk right now, I'm in a meeting.'

Damn! He'd really wanted to discuss this with her.

'Clint?' Gemini sounded as if she wasn't sure if he'd hung up yet.

'Yes?' he asked.

'I've got some news too - but it'll have to wait until I get home.'

'Give me a clue,' he said, unable to resist.

'Not now. Later,' she said. 'See you around six.'

Arriving home Clint parked his car and went inside and changed into his tracksuit and runners before racing outside again. The prospects of a new job excited him - nothing could dent his enthusiasm right now. After nine years with Benton Keenan Worldwide, he'd had enough of all the petty politics that happened in a multinational advertising agency.

Out in the brilliant sunshine Clint did some hamstring stretches and warm up exercises before starting his run. The truth was, it'd been five or more years since he'd got any real pleasure from his job. Not since he'd been involved in the early strategic meetings to launch a new biotech company had the job got his heart really pumping. Back then he'd helped his client raise twenty million dollars of public funds and worked with them, seeing their product marketed and the company grow until it was taken over by a multinational pharmaceutical company. Their projects had been satisfying, imaginative and fun - not like his current clients who bored him to near rigor mortis. There was a limit to how much excitement anyone could squeeze out of a rest home, a franchise of cosmetic surgeons, a health insurer, and a range of antifungal and dermatological preparations.

A car slowed to let him cross the road. With an extra skip he jumped onto the sidewalk and veered left, taking the track down to the beach, relaxing into an easy rhythm. The sea, he thought, was a good reminder of the transcience of life. And, while Gemini might tease him about having a mid-life crisis and he would deny it, he had to admit it was starting to bother him that the first thirty-eight years of his life had flashed by so quickly. *Exactly what had he done with them?*

The sand underfoot got firmer and Clint lengthened his stride, loving the free-flowing cadence of his arms and legs, the feeling of endorphins as they kicked in. He thought of Gemini and the salary review meeting she was to have that morning, and guessed she'd been successful, and that was her good news. Either that or she was pregnant, though he didn't think it would happen that soon. Besides, if he got this new job, it might be better to delay the baby plans, and if Gemini was able to earn a bit more, it would certainly help financially.

Leaving the beach, Clint crossed the road, deciding to take the long route back so he'd have more time to think things through. He remembered how they'd referred to his meeting this afternoon, as his *final* interview. Inuterogene - it was such an interesting company, just the sort of challenge he was looking for. Including the chance to work with Dr Katrina Dudek whose pioneering research in prenatal genetics had been honoured with the Watson Human Science Prize, the highest commendation awarded to innovators in the biotechnology field.

His first interview had been conducted by a firm of corporate headhunters, so it wasn't until his second interview that he met Dr Dudek for the first time. 'Please call me, Katrina,' she'd said, shaking his hand. Following her down the hallway to her office, he'd been surprised that she must only be close to forty, so young for someone so acclaimed.

They sat formally, facing each other across her desk. In her precise, business-like manner she explained the commercial sensitivity of the product before opening an envelope on her desk and taking out a thin piece of white plastic, no bigger than a credit card.

'This is a prototype of Invivotest,' she said, holding the plastic up for him to see. The card looked flat on both sides except for a small groove in the middle and a button on one edge. Katrina placed her index finger under the card and pushed the button, Clint heard a click and then saw Katrina squeeze her fingertip, forcing some blood onto the center of the card.

'It's that simple,' she said. 'Now all the customer has to do is send this card back to our laboratory and wait for us to process the results.'

'And how long does that take?'

'Just three hours from the moment we receive the card,' Katrina said. 'With Invivotest that's all that's required for any woman to get a full genetic profile of the growing fetus.'

'And the results are one-hundred percent reliable?'

'Yes,' she said.

Clint held his hand out and Katrina passed him the card. He clicked the button and watched a needle pop out and back. 'No need for a doctor, no risk of miscarriage. It's simplicity itself,' he said. 'Every woman will want to use it. To know the genetic destiny of your unborn child makes perfect sense.'

'Yes,' Katrina said, fixing her intense blue eyes on him.

'Well, I'm sold,' Clint said, before laughing at how silly he sounded. 'But then I'm not your target market!'

Katrina smiled. 'Not unless there's something you haven't told me.'

She was great! Clint knew then he could work for her, this was exactly the job he wanted to do. With four million babies born in the United States each year, the market potential was mind-boggling, it'd be an honor to be involved.

'What you need is someone to make Invivotest a household name. Someone prepared to make this a personal mission, I'm just the person you are looking for,' Clint said, infusing his voice with passion, every bit of which was genuine.

Slowing his pace, Clint walked the last ten minutes to his apartment. He was definitely looking forward to his interview this afternoon.

Clint heard the familiar grinding of the steel grills to the underground garage as they lifted to allow Gemini's white convertible entry. It was later than she'd promised, and he guessed she must have stayed for drinks after work - perhaps to celebrate her promotion.

Throwing her bag on the leather sofa, Gemini ran over and hugged him. Reaching up to kiss him, she thrust her tongue playfully into his mouth, teasing him, then pulled her head away. 'Have you guessed?' she asked, moving away.

'No, I didn't want to spoil your fun,' Clint said.

'I'm pregnant.'

There was a deafening pause. 'Oh,' he said.

'You could at least try to be a bit more excited,' she said. 'I thought you'd be over the moon.'

'I am,' he said. 'That's fantastic news it's just I didn't expect it would happen that quickly.'

'You've had all day to get excited - what other news did you think I had?'

'You told me you were having your review today. I thought you must have got a rise,' he added defensively. Sometimes he felt he shouldn't be so easily manipulated by her volatility.

She glared at him and he felt her fury. 'Trust you to only think about the money.'

'Be fair, Gemini, isn't that what you told me when you left this morning? Wasn't that a reasonable assumption?'

'Huh,' Gemini said, huffily. 'Even so, you still didn't sound very happy.'

'No, I didn't say that, it's just I was thinking that if I got that job it might've been good to wait a bit - '

Gemini turned her back on him and went to the kitchen to get a soda. Clint followed. ' - I was going to say something to you later, but it looks like the decision's already been made for us,' he said, knowing he was digging himself into deeper disapproval, wishing he wasn't so clumsy with his honesty.

He watched Gemini tilt her head back and take a long slow sip straight from the bottle and felt his mind dissolve; her beauty and fiery passion were like an addiction, she fed his soul. 'I didn't mean to sound anything other than happy,' he said, 'I'm overjoyed and I know it's what you want, it's what we both want, isn't it?'

She fixed her eyes on his, and in the space of three to four seconds he saw them soften then blur with forgiveness. Putting her drink on the bench, Gemini stepped towards Clint and he embraced her.

'Perhaps I can make it up to you,' he said, relieved she never seemed to hold a grudge for long. 'How about we go down and celebrate with one of Luigi's special pizzas?'

'You think you can buy me with a pizza, do you?'

'Can't I?'

'Well, okay, just this once, but first, you'll have to wait for me to get ready.'

In the shower Gemini savored the refreshing feeling of lukewarm water trickling down her spine. Letting her mind drift over the day's events, she stood mesmerised, watching water running down her thigh and off her knee before falling in an arc onto the white porcelain floor tiles.

She thought about her day. As a matter of fact she had managed a ten-percent pay-rise - but she wasn't going to tell him that, at least not yet. She decided she'd wait and see if he asked again, and then she smiled to herself - he wouldn't dare ask!

Turning the shower off she leant forward to squeeze the bulk of the water from her long hair then threw her hair back, flinging water droplets across the mirror and onto the wall tiles behind. The air movement jostled a mobile made from shells gathered on their honeymoon which hung now from the top of the windowsill according to feng shui principles, in a place that would bring them good fortune. She thought now that her pregnancy was proof the shells had been collected on a truly auspicious night.

Gemini sat at a table at the back of Luigi's pizza parlor listening to Clint rave on about Inuterogene. She was thinking how she'd never before seen him quite so animated by work. There was a sparkle in his eye that reminded her of the first time they met just over three years ago - at a pizzeria, one of the large franchised operations. She'd already ordered her Hawaiian to take out when he came in to order his. Something had drawn her to him, compelling her to make the first move, she asked him for some change to buy a drink from the vending machine. They struck up a conversation about the distinctive qualities of two famously branded cola's and the merits of their respective marketing strategies. It was, she knew, a peculiar subject to flirt over - she'd even thought that then - but it'd worked, and by the time their pizzas were ready Clint had asked her to join him at a table, and later that evening he asked her out another night.

Listening to him now she wondered which of the day's events meant the most to him: her pregnancy or his job?

'This could be my luckiest break yet,' he said. 'Worldwide the potential is *enormous*. If Invivotest is successful here in America we could launch in England, Europe, Australia, China, India. Imagine that!'

Gemini nodded, she could see how that would appeal to his

competitive streak though there was something almost naïve about his acceptance of the benefits of Invivotest, and that bothered her. Hadn't he thought about any of the negatives - or had his desperate boredom at work totally clouded his objectivity?

'I understand you're excited by this,' she said, 'but can't we talk about something else for a bit?'

'Sorry,' he said. 'I'm being boring, aren't I? Let's talk about the baby. How do you feel?'

Gemini smiled, her eyes suddenly filling with tears. She let out an embarrassed laugh. 'Very emotional,' she said. 'Overwhelmed, actually. Even though this is hardly unexpected, deep down I still never truly believed it would happen, that one day I would become a mother.' She stroked a tear away. 'This means so much to me, and the truth is I feel a bit jealous, and nervous, that your job will take your attention away from me and the baby,' she said, stroking her stomach.

'But why? You know you mean the world to me,' he said, reaching over running his hand down her cheek. 'You're the most important thing in my life.'

Gemini took his hand and traced her fingers over his before letting go. 'I know I'm being silly but I just wanted to hear you say it, that's all.'

A waiter came over and placed the pizza in front of them, then topped up their water glasses, the ice clinking noisily against the sides of the glass.

For a while they ate and chatted about other things, then Gemini relented and told Clint about her pay-rise.

'Congratulations, you deserve it,' Clint said.

They finished eating and the waiter cleared their plates. While they waited for dessert, Gemini decided to raise the issue of Clint's work.

'Had you given much thought to the downside of making the Invivotest available?' Gemini asked. 'There're going to be a lot of women who won't thank you for introducing it.'

'How do you mean?' Clint said.

'I was thinking about the pressure some women might face from partners to take the test, when they would rather not. And then there'll be those people who feel they have to take it just because it's available, causing them to worry about things they'd never thought of before.'

'Don't you think that's a small price to pay for the freedom women will experience if we prevent them having a baby that is disabled in some way? A baby that could ruin their lives.'

'You're assuming a life with a disability is worse than no life at all; what if they wanted the child anyway?' Gemini said.

'They can still have it.'

'Huh, that's easy for you to say. Some women will be blackmailed by their husbands to abort if they think there's even a chance their baby isn't going to be perfect. This test will become a way for men to control women's bodies.'

'But only with their say-so.'

Gemini stiffened. *Since when did women do a good job of sticking up for their rights?* 'Not true!' she said loudly. 'Everyone will have an opinion on who should be born and who shouldn't.'

'Well I think the benefits outweigh the drawbacks,' Clint said.

'I disagree. I think Invivotest *will* lead to women's bodies being seen as incubators.'

Clint shook his head and sighed. 'Don't you think you're being a little sexist here? It's never just the woman who suffers the burden of these decisions - '

'Get real, Clint! Of course it's the woman who suffers, we're the ones left holding the baby. The problem with tests like Invivotest is that, soon, any woman who gives birth to a genetically faulty baby will be blamed for having had it,' Gemini said, shuddering, visibly expressing her revulsion. 'Instead of receiving pity, she'll only receive judgement and guilt.'

She watched Clint take another bite of his dessert, and waited until she had eye contact. 'I can see the headlines now: Mother-in-law wins million-dollar lawsuit for deformed grandchild; Boy sues parents for time spent on handicapped baby sister; Child sues for genetic disabilities,' she said.

Clint noisily scraped the last of his tiramisu from the sides of his bowl and beckoned to the waiter for the bill. 'Perhaps for the time being we should just agree to disagree,' he said, pulling his jacket on, preparing to leave.

Gemini got in the car and turned on the radio, not wanting to talk. In her mind she debated whether it would be fair to ask Clint not to take the job if he were offered it. Yet he seemed so inspired - was it fair to deny him that challenge, and if she did, what effect would that have on their marriage long-term? From his point of view she could see why the job appealed - and it was true this was a unique opportunity - but all her instincts warned her against him getting involved. How could she let him know that without him accusing her of being manipulative? In the end she decided she would leave him to make up his own mind, with just one proviso.

'Clint,' she said gently, breaking the muse. 'Don't you feel our baby is a precious gift? From all the thousands of eggs I was born with and the many millions of sperm you donated, only two united and have already divided into a unique individual that no method of science could ever recreate. I wouldn't want to spoil the mystery of that miracle with a genetic profile taken before our baby's even born.'

'No one said you'd have to,' he replied.

Arriving home, Clint turned the engine off and reached across and felt for her hand in the dark. 'I promise.'

In the darkened car, Gemini sensed his empathy, and knew there was never going to be a better time. 'No matter how much you might want to - will you promise me one thing?' she said, not daring to look at him. 'Promise me you'll never ask me to take the Invivotest on our baby.'

Several minutes went by before Clint spoke again, and when he did Gemini thought how it sounded like a switch had been flicked and he'd been transformed into work-mode. 'The thing is, the pragmatist in me can't help but want to try and improve on nature's failure rate. Nature can be cruel at times; why shouldn't we improve things where we can?'

'And you make it all sound so logical,' Gemini said, 'but to my way of thinking Invivotest doesn't improve on nature - it criticises it. And then provides us with the temptation to intervene and play God.'

Katrina Dudek stood in front of the floor-to-ceiling window, her shoulders square, legs apart. From the forty-second floor of Windsor Tower the cityscape stretched before her like a tile mosaic. Away in the farthest distance the city buildings smudged into a bland pastiche of faded yellows and browns, the Californian sun scorching around the desert edges of the city.

Squinting against the hazy glare of the afternoon sky, she watched a helicopter landing on a rooftop a few buildings in front. The passenger door opened, and a dark-haired man scurried out. Steen Davis had arrived.

She smiled to herself, enjoying the incongruity of seeing Steen Davis duck for cover - few people would have seen him from this angle, trousers flattened against his legs, suit tails billowing in the wind.

Going back to her desk she picked up a glass paperweight and twirled it in the palm of her hand. Turning the glass globe she watched the silver point of the compass needle shimmer right and left before returning to its north position. It'd once been David's compass, used on science fiction expeditions in their backyard. For many years, driving space rockets with Scott had been their favorite game. David would navigate with his map and compass while Katrina would battle aliens on their journey to Mars, and when Scott was around he'd be recruited for his experience as an extra-terrestrial physicist.

The helicopter lifted off the ground behind her, passing close to the window. Katrina sensed its nearness and turned her head in time to catch a glimpse of the pilot's reflective goggles and earmuffs.

Two seconds later the chopper banked and swooped away, its blades urgently scything through the skies and out of sight.

Katrina set the paperweight back on her desk, it held so many memories but one in particular eclipsed all others. David standing, King Neptune-like, with a garden rake in one hand and a steel bucket on his head. 'We are masters of our destiny and captains of our souls,' he'd said, just as there was a loud ding, the sound of excrement falling from a bird that flew overhead.

David! Most of what she'd done with her life was because of him. She looked out the window and guessed that by now Steen would've entered the hushed elevator on the top of the Royal Grand Hotel. She could imagine him standing, impeccable head held high, suave as ever, staring ahead as the doors slammed shut. When they were closed he would smooth his hair, check his image in the glass panel, and quickly adjust his tie just seconds before the doors opened again.

Next he would head straight towards the revolving glass-and-brass-trimmed circular doors, across the granite floor and stride on out into the jewel-blue summer's day. He would walk one block, cross at the lights, and enter the cool bank vault-like chambers of Windsor Tower where, after a thorough screening procedure, security would escort him to an express elevator at the rear of the building. Once the floor was keyed in, Steen would be rushed to his final destination, level forty-two.

Katrina opened the top drawer of her desk, some coins slid across the wooden lining, and a pen, lipstick, and gold compact rolled to the back. She checked her makeup and reapplied some lipstick.

The phone rang again. This time it was her secretary. 'Shall I take Steen through to the boardroom?'

'Thank you, Sarah. Give him a coffee, and let me know when Randall and Lisa arrive.'

She checked her watch knowing she could count on Randall and Lisa being at least ten minutes late. Randall was a partner in the esteemed legal firm Cripp Jones, his area of special interest corporate finance and taxation; Lisa was an associate partner and an expert in securities. They'd attended to the legal details of the dissolution of the current joint venture partnership and the re-incorporation of Inuterogene as an independent company.

That this was to be the last of a marathon series of meetings haggling over the most equitable deal was almost unbelievable - for the past twelve months it seemed as though she'd done nothing else.

Sarah knocked on the door and poked her head into the room. 'They're here now, are you ready?'

Katrina nodded, she was as ready now as she ever would be. She was about to sign the documents that would give her the fifty million dollars of venture capital she needed to see her dreams fly. Fifty million was, she thought, a consummate show of confidence in her abilities; not bad for a girl who left home at the age of seventeen, pregnant with twins.

Sarah waited outside the boardroom. 'Do you need me in there?' she asked.

'No, that won't be necessary,' Katrina replied, maneuvering her way past. Steen rose as she approached, smiling reservedly, his Bahamas' holiday-bronzed skin made his blue eyes look almost bleached of color by contrast. She shook his hand, noticing its warmth and softness, like a child's - he obviously didn't spend his weekends cutting the grass and cleaning leaves from drainpipes.

'Katrina, great to see you again,' he said.

She returned his greeting and nodded to Randall and Lisa, sensing that none of them had had enough time to establish any small talk; she presumed they'd all be tense, each having invested a lot of time and effort in this project.

Katrina took a chair at the far end of the boardroom table, with her back to the window. 'Thanks for making us a priority, Steen. I know how busy you are,' she said. 'I have it on good authority that Zenogen is closer to launch than we originally thought. While we've got regulatory approval before they have, we can't afford to become complacent; we have to recover more than one hundred million in research and development costs before we even start to see a profit.' Her eyes rested on Steen's. 'Do you think we're finally ready?'

Steen responded with a smile that was part grimace, part grunt. 'I think so. I've got the release signatures from the joint-venture partners, so now we're just waiting on your approval.'

'You've done a great job,' she said, meaning it, knowing how many long frustrating hours he'd spent in negotiations with each of the partners to get them to agree to this settlement.

Steen opened his briefcase and pulled out a cream-colored folder. He passed the documents around the table before directing his audience to the relevant pages. A hush fell on the room as they studied the papers in front of them. Outside, in the reception area, Katrina could hear the phones ringing.

Randall looked up. 'I'm satisfied. What about you, Lisa?'

Lisa nodded. 'I'm happy.'

'In that case if you'd like to witness and sign the marked changes, we'll be able to conclude this business,' Steen said.

For a while the only noise in the room was the scratch of pens and crackle of paper. One set of documents finalised Steen's admission to the board and the stockholding of Davis Venture Capital Co. Inc. in exchange for its fifty million debenture; the other set formalised Katrina's new responsibilities as chairperson of the board and chief executive officer of the newly-structured company.

'We look forward to great things from our association with you, Katrina,' Steen said, his eyes communicating nothing except an absence of emotion. 'How about we celebrate in the customary fashion; let's say dinner at seven?'

Katrina closed the gilt-edged menu, casting her eyes round the room to check there was no one there she knew.

Steen reached under the table then passed her a lavishly wrapped gift. Taking it from him, she felt a swoosh of panic, stumbling to find the words to protest his generosity.

'It's a token,' he said, 'nothing really, just something special to celebrate.'

Her mind whirred: what did he expect from her now? Surely this was only a business relationship?

Undoing the black satin ribbon, she tore away the matt black paper to reveal a polished wooden-box. She opened it and pulled out a gold pen with an eagle engraved along its side, two rows of tiny diamonds inset into each extended wing, glittered in the light. She turned it around and saw an inscription: *May you fly to greater heights. Steen.*

For a few moments she couldn't see anything for the blur of tears that filled her eyes. It struck her then that no one else had supported her achievement so personally; and that there was no one else to share it with.

'You've embarrassed me,' she said. 'You shouldn't have bought me anything at all.'

'It was my pleasure,' he said.

The wine waiter brought champagne to the table and Steen proposed a toast. 'Here's to our bright new future,' he said, raising his glass, taking a sip, smacking his lips. 'In fact, I think the timing is perfect. I'm picking the stock market is on the way up and we want to catch that wave because every now and again there are windows of opportunity when the market is hot for new stocks. In the heat of a fad, stocks sell well above market value with virtually no effort at all. But when the stocks are out of fashion, they'll create about as much interest from investors as a cold plate of spaghetti.'

She knew he was putting pressure on her; to him time was money. Now he'd closed one deal he'd be in a hurry to do the next. Until Inuterogene listed on the stock exchange, Davis Venture Capital Co. Inc. would have no way of showing a return on their investment. He had to turn a profit. She knew that.

Steen stopped talking while the waiter refilled their champagne glasses. When they were alone again he continued, 'Today's fifty million won't go far, you're going to need a successful public offering or you'll soon be undercapitalised, and we don't want that.'

'No, we don't want that,' she said, mocking his tone.

'In fact it might be wise to consider incorporating an anti-takeover strategy into the company's charter - we could devise two classes of common stock.'

'That sounds like a good idea,' she said, grateful for his cautionary advice, for though she had the largest stockholding it wasn't a majority. He knew as well as she did, she had her lifetime's work at stake. 'But wouldn't the market resist that sort of a set-up?'

He shrugged. 'If we create enough competition for our business amongst the underwriters we'll probably get away with it. Besides, people are less cautious when the market's heating up.'

'In that case let's do it,' she said.

'We'll also need to strengthen the Board,' he said.

'But I like the Board the way it is,' she said, giving him a conspiratorial smile, knowing he was aware she'd picked all the current board members herself, and that they would give her their full support on all the issues that really mattered. 'So why do we need to change?'

'To meet the requirements of the stock exchange we must have at least three board members who are completely independent,' Steen explained.

'Oh, I see,' she teased. 'No wonder you wanted to give me time to consider it.'

'Seriously Katrina, you need to think about this. If we can attract some big names to the Board there'll be lots of advantages - it'll act as a magnet for free publicity and good staff, not to mention the boost in confidence it'd give the market. If you like I could help you, I know some people who'd be ideal.'

'Thanks, I'd appreciate your help,' she said, interrupted by the waiter bringing their food. Deconstructing the chef's handiwork, Steen proceeded to tell her what else he'd help her with. The appointment of underwriters; registration with the Securities and Exchange; due diligence; the preparation of a prospectus; and a plan to promote their stocks to the financial markets.

- 9 -

At the sound of a knock on her office door, Gemini looked up to see her receptionist bringing in a huge bunch of yellow roses.

'Aren't they lovely! Is it a special occasion?'

Gemini said nothing.

'The newlyweds have a slight lovers' tiff, did they?' persisted the receptionist, lifting one eyebrow mockingly.

'You could say that,' Gemini said. 'We didn't agree on something, but that's men for you, isn't it? I'm sure they're from a different planet - they just can't seem to appreciate anything without putting a value on it first.'

The receptionist laid the flowers on Gemini's desk. 'Well, at least you got those, and if you don't enjoy them you'll be no better than they are.'

Gemini unclipped the card. *Sorry for being an ass, love you truly, madly, deeply, C.*

Smiling to herself, she hit speed dial, and when she was put through to his voice mail she left a message. 'Thanks for the flowers. You're forgiven, but only just. See you about seven. Bye for now.'

Turning her mind back to work, Gemini mentally prepared herself for her next client meeting with the manufacturer of a range of vitamin supplements whose business had been sabotaged by an employee who had mixed rat poison into some of the pills. In her opinion there was no hope customer confidence could be regained. While no one had been hurt by the malicious act, the publicity generated by the product recall had done irreparable damage. She had no choice but to recommend they rename the product. In the business world there is no such thing as loyalty - three years as an account manager in a market research company had taught her that.

Gemini was pleased when it was time to leave work, all day she'd been bothered by nausea and hadn't eaten. Once home she was able to satisfy her craving for tuna. Taking her sandwich and the newspaper out onto the balcony, she turned to the art section and read an article on Garth Rodwell, her favorite artist. Only last year she'd bought a signed print of his famed Yellow Tortoise. Giving it to Clint as a present she was disappointed he'd been less enamored with the mystical picture that still sat, abandoned and unframed in one corner of their home office.

Thinking of Clint, she ran her fingertips over the gold scalloped-shell locket that hung from her neck. Closing her eyes, she tuned into the romantic resonance of her honeymoon gift, smiling inwardly, knowing how Clint would laugh if she told him the shell had good karma and that it was a spiritual connection with him and his new baby in the making. Nothing - she believed - happens by accident. She'd studied Carl Jung and his theory on synchronicities at university and since then she'd often argued with Clint that it wasn't chance that had brought them together the night they first met, though he would say it was.

Katrina completed her final lap in the rooftop pool. The night skies were a darkened blue, lighting from surrounding tower blocks shimmering through the smoggy haze. Climbing out of the pool, she picked her kimono off a deck chair and fastened the belt before taking the elevator back to her apartment on the twenty-third floor.

Stepping inside, she turned on the television and settled into the black leather sofa to watch the news - a gun massacre in a shopping mall, an oil spill in the Pacific Ocean, then the item she was waiting for. Behind the newsreader appeared a picture of a serpent entwined around a double-helix DNA ladder, two large yellow dollar signs inside its eyes. Pointing the remote at the screen she turned the volume up.

'Pregnant women will soon be able to buy a home-test kit to predict the genetic status of their newly conceived baby. According to the developers - Zenogen - this new test will be particularly relevant for women at risk of conceiving children with some of the major genetic defects such as Down Syndrome, muscular dystrophy, hemophilia, Huntington's chorea, cystic fibrosis, Tay-Sachs and multiple sclerosis.'

The newsreader blinked benignly as the snake's head disappeared and a weather map came on screen. Katrina switched the television off and plugged in her laptop computer, wondering how Zenogen would be ready to be launched so soon.

Entering the Zenogen website address she looked for confirmation of the product and release dates and found none, only teaser anecdotes and vague verbal commendations about a brand-new unnamed test that would be 'particularly relevant' for some pregnant women.

Surely they're bluffing, they must be!

Out of curiosity she clicked on the icon for investor information and checked the prices. Today's high: $28. Today's low: $23.

A five-dollar gain in one day - that's got to be good news for someone.

- 10 -

Gemini stood by the balcony railing staring across the calm sea as it glistened under the luminous quarter moon. Below her she could see a stream of yellow and red lights as Newport commuters whizzed past her apartment block on their way home, or out for a night on the town. It was ten past *eight*. Damn him, why couldn't he be early just this once?

Since Clint had started his new job nearly two weeks ago she'd hardly seen him. Gemini punched the buttons on the remote control, switching channels every few seconds only to find nothing of interest, clicking it off in irritation.

The moment she heard Clint on the landing outside she leapt from the sofa and was at the door before it opened. Clint struggled in, his arms piled high with a briefcase and several folders spilling papers out the sides, and under his chin was tucked a bunch of flowers that were slowly falling from his grasp.

'Oh, Clint, you shouldn't have,' Gemini said as she rescued the bouquet.

He dumped his files on the kitchen table and started sorting them into piles. Gemini found a vase and took the flowers into the lounge, placing them on a large wooden coffee table in the middle of the room. She closed the shoji doors to the hallway and switched on a Japanese lantern that filtered softly diffused light up the wall. Happy with the ambience she'd created, she went back to the kitchen, noticing with pleasure how warm the terracotta tiles felt underfoot. She liked the stabilising effect the tiles had on the chi in the room, and despite what Clint had said at the time they *were* worth the extra wait and inconvenience.

Gemini ushered Clint into the lounge. Taking their dinner plates through on trays they sat on the sofa together in the peaceful quietness, Clint scooping his chicken and rice down in large mouthfuls.

'Yum, that was delicious, thank you,' he said, moving his plate to one side before trying to kiss her. 'You know, it's true what they say about those pregnancy hormones, you're looking radiant tonight. Quite desirable if I - '

'Don't.' Gemini moved out of his reach.

'What is it?' A hurt look flickered across Clint's face, making her regret being so brusque.

'I went to the doctor today, it's probably nothing, but he wants me to go for a scan tomorrow.' Gemini felt her eyes fill with tears; she'd wanted to tell him matter-of-factly but her emotions had leaked to the surface. Trying to steady her voice, she managed to say, 'We might be having twins. How do you feel about that?'

'Wonderful!' he said. 'I guess we'll just have to hope they don't fight like you and Hudson did!'

Gemini let out a tremulous laugh. He was going to make a great dad, of that she was sure.

'The scan's at ten. You'll be there - just in case?' she asked. 'This pregnancy means so much to me I can't help feeling worried. What if something's not right with our baby?'

Clint said nothing; instead he moved towards her and held her close, as if he knew how much she wanted to feel his strength, and calm.

The medical clinic was a multi-storied glass tower with architectural steel scaffolding on the outside, and a glass dome on the top that made it look more like a long-legged spacecraft from *War of the Worlds* than a medical center.

Inside the building, Gemini took a seat beside the water cooler and Clint stood in one corner studying some booklets contained in a revolving file, no doubt critiquing the marketing Gemini thought.

Some silver fish flitted through reeds and anemone tentacles in a designer aquarium that bubbled against the wall.

'Eight,' she said.

Clint gave her a quizzical look.

'I counted eight fish, that's auspicious,' she said.

'Good,' he said, replacing a brochure just as a nurse called Gemini's name. They followed the nurse to a room where Dr Stone greeted them before asking Gemini to climb onto the examination table.

Pulling a trolley with an ultrasound scanner close to him, the doctor picked up a bottle of lubricant and dribbled some over Gemini's stomach. He smoothed the head of the ultrasonic transducer over her rounded midriff and some images appeared on the computer screen.

The obstetrician worked silently and Gemini stared at the incomprehensible blobs and slithery lines that moved like a dynamic meteorological chart. 'Congratulations,' he eventually said. 'You're having twins.'

Despite her twin brother and the likelihood of this possibility all along, it was still a shock. Gemini swallowed hard. Clint had gone pale but was smiling; she couldn't tell what he was thinking - hell, she couldn't even tell what she was thinking.

Turning her attention back to the computer monitor Gemini tried once more to identify which parts of the swirling meteors were her babies, but her eyes refused to focus and everything became a blur - suddenly the pregnancy was real, those were living images, her flesh and blood.

'Ah, gotcha!' said the doctor, freeze-framing one of the twins, his face relaxing as he critiqued the stationary image on the screen. Happy with his catch, he fixed some vector points and took the baby's measurements - head circumference, femur length, kidneys, stomach, bladder. Releasing that picture he captured another image, a small pulsing blob. He tapped a command on his keyboard, enlarging the image of the baby's heart, 'Perfect,' he muttered. A few seconds later he asked Gemini to change position so he could find the second baby and repeat the procedure. Less than five minutes later he was finished.

'That all looks fine,' Dr Stone said, pressing a button to turn the monitor off. He helped Gemini get down from the bed 'I'd like to see you again in a fortnight's time. It seems one of our new friends might be growing at a slower rate. No need to be alarmed, but I think we should check just to be on the safe side.'

He showed them to the door. Stunned, Gemini finally found her voice to ask, 'But I want to know, is something wrong?'

'It's too early to tell,' he said, looking past Gemini's eyes, smiling vaguely at the wall.

- 11 -

Clint didn't see the red traffic light until it was too late. He put his foot down and accelerated in front of the cars that had started to cross the road. Grateful no harm was done, he cursed his inattention, knowing he'd been preoccupied with thoughts about work, and Gemini and the twins.

Every day he was confronted with statistics on infant imperfections, and ever since the scan, it was getting hard not to let his imagination run away with him but he knew it would be unfair, and there was no point sharing his concerns with Gemini. With no other choice he pushed his fears to the back of his mind; he was just going to have to learn how to stop being paranoid.

He pulled off the expressway into the San Remo Industrial Estate, a new commercial zone, much preferring this location to the inner-city building he'd been interviewed in. Here all the properties were larger than fifty hectares, some up to two hundred and most had a recreational facility - a golf course, swimming pool, gymnasium, or tennis court of some sort. The buildings were uniformly low-rise, made of stone or brick with terracotta tile roofing; there was no corrugated iron in this neighborhood. These were the headquarters of many big name multinationals where business ideas were hatched and strategies bankrolled. Only a few had warehouse facilities - for here, raw materials and production schedules were mainly managed by e-mail, and business-class travel to factories in either third-world countries or out of state.

Clint pulled into the Inuterogene driveway, feeling a sense of awe knowing the perfectly manicured lawns had been trucked in only days ago, arriving with an automated sprinkling system guaranteed to keep the grass emerald-green despite the Californian sun. In keeping with the overall theme, the cobbled drive was lined with twenty-three pairs of phoenix palms, one for each chromosomal pair.

He parked his car and looked over at the water fountain that was still under construction. A magnificent piece of artwork, the fountain was made of thick glass spiral tubes that wrapped around an aluminum centerpiece imitating the double-helix structure of DNA. Clint knew that as soon as the workmen had finished attaching the night lights to the inside of the marble base, the pump would be turned on so water could flow from the top of the structure, down around its winding curves. He looked forward to seeing that.

Standing outside the entrance to the building he took his security card and swiped it through the black box, waiting for the glass doors to unlock and slide open with an electronic purr. He crossed the slate tiles and Sarah greeted him with a stack of messages, including one from Gemini reminding him to meet her at the medical center that afternoon.

'Oh, and there's a message from Katrina,' Sarah said. 'She won't be coming in today, but she'll see you tonight. She said don't go to any trouble, she'll order in some pizzas - does that make any sense to you?'

Clint nodded; he'd nearly forgotten he'd invited Katrina around for a drink that evening.

Gemini parked her car outside the medical clinic. For the past two weeks Clint had been so absorbed by work he'd barely mentioned the babies; yet for her it had been a long fourteen days, possibly the longest ever. Everywhere she'd gone there were babies, playgrounds, shops with infant clothing, aisles of toys, baby foods, diapers. Even smells had invaded her life - petrol, exhaust fumes and fatty foods all made her want to retch, reminding her of the new lives growing within her.

Each time she recalled the scan she felt a leap of joy at the memory of the babies' images, but then the happiness would be followed almost instantaneously by fear, guilt and conflict. Should she have done more to find out about her genetic history? For the sake of her babies, did she now have an obligation? Or are some things in life best left to chance?

There seemed to be no right answer.

Though she never told Clint, she even reconsidered doing the Invivotest but then dismissed the idea - if the results showed something wrong it would only spoil the pregnancy, especially if there was no cure. In a small way, she'd already compromised her objection to prenatal tests by agreeing to the ultrasound scan but the scan, she rationalised, was routine - all doctors, scared of malpractice suits, recommended them. Besides, it was purely observational, an important distinction from Invivotest whose results are conclusive.

Seeing Clint pull into the car park Gemini waited for him to join her. She admired the way he had never once gone back on his word and asked her to do the Invivotest, it was almost like an unspoken trade - he'd swapped her permission to take the job in exchange for her right not to Invivotest the babies.

When Clint was near he half-jogged, half-skipped the last few steps, looking as though he didn't have a care in the world. Leaning forwards to kiss him, she thought he seemed happy, perhaps a little on the exaggerated side.

With a nod towards her convertible, he said, 'It'll ruin your image, but I'm afraid that's going to have to go. We'll have to trade it in for something far more sedate!'

'I suppose you think I need something really boring now I'm about to become a mother of two,' she said, playfully smacking him.

'Just so long as you don't drive around with a bag of disposable diapers in the rear window, I'm not having that!' he said.

When they got inside the building they found it was virtually empty. They were told to take a seat, and out of force of habit Gemini recounted the fish. She thought there were six this time, still a lucky number she told Clint.

The nurse led them down the hallway then left them with Dr Stone who finished writing his notes before showing Gemini to the examination table. The doctor switched on the ultrasound, studying the images that emerged on the screen. Clint stared at the monitor, his face offering no clues to his thoughts. He appeared so normal, so clinically objective, Gemini thought enviously - but then he could, none of this was happening inside *him*.

After what seemed like forever, the doctor finally spoke. 'Your babies are fine,' he said. 'I don't see anything anatomically wrong with either, though one is definitely smaller, it may just be a tiny baby.'

Outside in the car park Clint gave Gemini a delighted hug. 'What a relief!' he said, letting out some joyous whoops. Opening Gemini's car door, Clint bowed and swept his hand in front of his chest. 'Madam.'

'Why, thank you kind sir,' Gemini said, throwing him a coy look before climbing in.

Clint checked his watch then leant over to kiss goodbye. 'I'd better get a move on, I've got a meeting in fifteen minutes,' he said.

Gemini watched him leave, feeling a pang of pathos that his attention was so quickly diverted. On the way home she stopped to buy some groceries, and on impulse bought some diapers, planning to put the roof down and jam them behind the seat and take Clint for a drive when he got home, they both could do with a good laugh.

- 12 -

Gemini was annoyed that Clint got home too late to go for a drive, he only had time for a quick shower before Katrina arrived.

Clint went inside to fix some drinks, leaving Gemini and Katrina sitting on the balcony in the slowly advancing dusk. For a few moments they sat and watched some joggers on the street below, the reflectors on their shoes glinting in the headlights of a passing car.

'Do you have any family?' Gemini asked.

'No,' Katrina said simply.

The single word politely, but definitely, stopped that conversation dead leaving Gemini to search for another topic they might have in common. Worried Clint would return to find them sitting in an inhospitable silence, she picked the first subject she knew would guarantee a reply. 'What inspired you to develop Invivotest?' she asked conversationally.

'I wanted to give parents a choice about the quality of life they are to bring into the world,' Katrina said. 'Not everyone can provide the amount of love that is needed to look after a child with a disability.'

Gemini nodded, she'd hoped for a slightly longer reply.

'But surely some people don't know how much love they have to give until they are put in that situation?' Gemini said.

'True in some cases,' Katrina said. 'But there are others who've already experienced the hardship and suffering of something like autism, and they know they couldn't raise a child like that, so why should they?'

Clint reappeared and Gemini took the drink he handed her. 'But with cheaper and easier testing won't everyone feel obliged to test -

and is it fair then to raise doubt over every fetus, to view them all as a liability?' Gemini sipped her drink. 'Is it fair to make every parent face that decision?'

'If the technology exists, is it fair not to?' Katrina replied, taking a drink from the tray Clint was holding.

Gemini shrugged. 'It just seems wrong somehow, we already score everything in our lives with marks out of ten, and now, Invivotest will even allow us to do that to the unborn.'

Clint put down the tray and pulled up his chair.

'I see nothing wrong with giving parents advance information,' Katrina said.

'Except that information could be self-fulfilling,' Gemini said. 'It could become a life sentence. You can't expect parents to keep an open mind when the information you provide is so accurate, so intensely personal - '

'A bit like some of the things that are being said now,' said Clint, ignoring Gemini's stare, his eyes fixed on Katrina. 'Gemini and I have often debated what constitutes human nature and we can never agree,' he said, speaking for the pair of them as if they'd been married twenty years, not less than one. 'For example, I think it's in our nature to be competitive and that it is one of mankind's greatest strengths but Gemini argues competition leads to aggression and violence and we can evolve just as well without it. '

'Actually I think human nature arguments are a cop out. They're used to stifle change and defend the status quo,' Gemini said, noting the faint smile on Katrina's face - a patronising smile, she thought, but then what can you expect when your husband starts to do the talking for you?

A loud buzz from the intercom sounded in the background and Clint made no effort to move. When it buzzed impatiently a second time, Gemini went to answer the door. In a while she came back carrying two large pizza boxes that she placed on the table before heading back inside to fetch some plates.

When she returned Clint and Katrina were absorbed in the details of a clinical trial so she sat down quietly, glad of the chance to simply observe. It irritated her to see how alert and responsive Clint appeared, his intellectual passion for work inspiring him in a way nothing else did.

After a while Clint pushed some pizza in Gemini's direction, breaking her reverie. 'You felt relieved after the scan, didn't you, Gem?'

'Hmmm,' she said, aware this might be leading towards a viewpoint she didn't care for. 'So?'

'Peace of mind. Most people will get results that tell them their baby is okay. That's what our marketing should focus on - the ninety-nine percent who've got nothing to worry about, rather than the one percent who do.'

'Don't you think you're deluding yourself? You can't tell me you weren't worried these last couple of weeks,' Gemini said, thinking of her own experience over the last two weeks, thinking as a mother. 'I'm sure anyone who does your test will live in fear, like I did after the scan. Until they get their results back, their minds will be focused on all the 'what if' scenarios: What if my baby has cystic fibrosis? What if it has Down Syndrome, or there's something else wrong with it?'

Gemini looked at Clint; he was staring at her, unblinking, his eyes warning her to back off. She guessed this discussion was getting too personal by his standards - but they were his babies too, how could he not agree with her?

Clint acted as if he may not have heard.

'Clint?' she said, more loudly this time. 'The last two weeks, did that honestly feel like peace of mind?'

'No,' he said eventually.

The night had darkened and Gemini couldn't see his face, it was hard to tell if he was embarrassed, annoyed, or simply collecting his thoughts. 'I rest my case,' she said softly.

'Not exactly,' Katrina said. 'All you've done is present a convincing case for early testing and immediate results - '

Gemini interrupted. 'But testing at six weeks? I don't call that peace of mind, I call that paranoia; some of those babies will be sucked out of existence before they've even had chance to twiddle their thumbs.'

'Except in the early weeks, not everyone sees that tiny collusion of cells as a baby, in fact some would argue they were just a lump of genetic material that had taken the body hostage,' Katrina said.

'Some might argue that, but I would rate them as sorry, heartless individuals,' Gemini said, blurting it out without thinking, realising she might have just got personal. She stopped and looked in Clint's direction; his silhouette seemed even more statuesque.

Gemini turned to Katrina. 'I'm sure that's not what you think, is it, Doctor?' she asked, her voice withering away, suddenly regretting she might have gone too far; soon they'd be a one-income family and this woman controlled their livelihood.

Katrina straightened in her seat, and for a moment Gemini thought she was going to leave. Panic raced through her veins and she looked at Clint, or at least his profile; he still hadn't moved, not an inch. She wondered what he'd say when they were alone that night.

'I guess it depends on when you think those cells assume the rights of a person,' Katrina said. 'When is that defining moment? Is it when the egg is first fertilised? Or when the brain first appears, the heart starts pumping, or later, when the fetus has the ability to breathe unassisted?'

Gemini shrugged, unable to think, feeling only relief, and the blood pulse in her veins again. 'I don't know,' she said. 'When do you think that moment is?'

Katrina sipped her coffee, then answered obtusely. 'It doesn't matter what I think but a lot depends on when other people think that moment is,' she said. 'Because as soon as we call the fetus a *baby* we move into a whole new dimension of emotionalism.'

Gemini nodded. 'I understand your point, but the decision to have a baby, or not, strikes at the heart of humanity - and I already worry about the lack of compassion in our society... I don't quite know why I care so much, unless it has something to do with the fact I was adopted.' She suddenly felt tearful and was glad that in the dark, if she kept control of her voice, it would not be noticeable. 'It's entirely possible that with a different mother we could have been terminated; we might never have existed.'

'We?' asked Katrina.

'I have a twin brother.'

Just then the breeze got up and it seemed like as good a time as any to move inside.

All three had to squint to refocus their vision under the harsh electric lighting. Gemini noticed how tired Clint looked; it had been a long emotional day for them both so she was thankful when Katrina made noises about leaving.

'Pregnancy is more tiring than I expected,' agreed Gemini, showing Katrina to the door. 'Thanks for coming. I hope I didn't cause any offense.'

Katrina murmured she'd taken none, and while Gemini waited for her to put on her jacket she realised - as if the sentiments came from the babies themselves - why she had such strong reservations about the Invivotest. 'It's just that now I'm pregnant it's confirmed my innermost feeling that having a baby is an act of love, it's a decision that should be made with the heart, not the mind.'

'I guess that's where we differ,' Katrina said. 'To me, it's a decision that should be made by the head.'

Gemini turned to Clint. 'What do you think, Clint - head or heart?'

Clint stood transfixed, on his face a look of utter helplessness and despair; how could he please both women? Pretending to faint, Clint threw his hands in the air, and Gemini and Katrina laughed, letting him off the hook.

- 13 -

Thirty-one-year-old Jackson Forrester hated talking in front of a group. The president of operations, Jackson was what Katrina would call a man's man - better with a work schedule, a container load of boxes and a forklift driver than he was with words. He sourced materials, arranged tenders and shipping, and was responsible for all the factory operations and production staff.

Before he joined Inuterogene he'd worked with one of the biggest computer wholesalers in the USA and had visited almost all the larger silicon chip and computer component factories in Taiwan, China, Korea and Japan. There wasn't much he didn't know about new DNA chip technology, corrupt business deals and dodgy oriental food markets.

The data display projected some figures onto a screen at the front of the boardroom and Katrina tuned in again to hear what he was saying. 'According to Katrina's sales estimates, if we open our distribution channels to include supermarkets and other stores we'll need an extra ten to twelve weeks to give us enough time to produce the extra stock.'

Katrina interrupted. 'Brandon, did you run those calcs on price?'

Her finance manager nodded and opened the leather folder placed in front of him. Passing around some spreadsheets he explained the likely outcomes of different price options. Jackson switched off the projection unit and sat down.

Katrina scanned the faces in the room, Brandon's words skimming over her head. She knew all the pricing options off by heart and took comfort in the knowledge that whichever option they chose they would always be cheaper than any other test currently available. Recalling the meeting she and Brandon had attended with the regulatory authorities, although they had submitted tonnes of irrefutable scientific documentation, she knew it was their pricing proposal that won them approval.

Tuning back into Brandon's words she heard him summarise the main points of his talk: The retail price of Invivotest would affect demand, and an increased demand would lower the price, with both affecting profitability. By his estimates, sales volumes could be up to ten times greater if Invivotest was sold in all stores without restriction.

Brandon stopped talking and Katrina thanked him.

'So there we have it,' she said, 'we all want to beat Zenogen to market but first we have to be clear about our strategy. Do we limit potential sales, and profitability, by selling exclusively through doctors or do we sell Invivotest in all stores with no restrictions?'

Looking round the room Katrina saw Michael Cookson, her head scientist, fiddling with his pen appearing not to want to comment.

Jackson spoke first. 'I don't think we should pussy-foot around, there's obviously more money to be made by going direct.'

'I agree, I'm all for going direct,' Brandon said.

'Does this have to be an either-or decision; why can't we do both?' asked Dwayne, head of information technology.

'Because doctors like exclusivity,' Brandon said, 'that way they can hike the price.'

'Exclusivity sounds risky to me,' Jackson said.

'We'd have difficulty getting our volumes up if they overcharged,' Clint agreed.

Dr Stefano Silvano, the medical affairs officer, the eldest of the group, raised a finger indicating his desire to speak. 'You can't go direct to the consumer and expect doctors to support you on that,' he said with disdain.

'Obviously we have to resolve this issue before we can move on,' Katrina said. 'Let's put it to the vote: All those in favor of marketing direct to the public raise their hands.'

Clint, Jackson and Brandon lifted their hands.

'Three plus my vote, four,' Katrina said. 'Hands up all those in favor of exclusive distribution rights to the medical profession.'

Dr Silvano raised his hand.

Katrina tallied out loud, 'One.'

She looked at Dwayne and Michael then said, 'And all those that don't know?'

Dwayne and Michael raised their hands.

'Obviously some of us still need a bit more time to come round to my way of thinking,' she said. But no one laughed.

'No chance,' Dr Silvano said. Katrina forced a smile, she knew she wouldn't change his mind but in the end it wouldn't matter, provided she won a two-vote majority.

'How much more time do the 'don't knows' need?' she asked, making it clear that anyone who hadn't made his mind up by now was beneath contempt. 'Dwayne, Michael? Do I need to remind you of the urgency of this decision? Perhaps we can reconvene for a vote on this tomorrow?'

Everyone murmured or nodded some form of agreement and Katrina declared the meeting over.

Stopping by the water cooler on her way back to her office she took a glass of water back to her desk and picked up her phone messages, her mind on other matters. What did she have to do to get Dwayne and Michael to see her point of view?

Clearly she'd misjudged Dwayne - how often did she have to learn that lesson: to never take anything for granted? Though they'd worked together since the early days when she'd commissioned him to develop the gene-decoding software, familiarity had led her to assume she knew his opinions when she'd never really checked with him.

He appeared happy in his job, she wondered why he should care whether Invivotest was sold directly to the public or not. Knowing he had three ex-wives and three children to support she knew money was important to him. She decided to pay him a visit, make him take a closer look at the spreadsheets, perhaps *then* he'd see how much more rewarding things would be.

And Michael? She sighed; he was far more complicated. For one thing, money didn't motivate him. He was already wealthy when she lured him from one of the biggest biotech companies listed on the NASDAQ exchange. He'd been attracted by the opportunity to be the biggest fish in a small pond, and for the challenge of seeing the company grow.

Katrina frowned. Unlike Dwayne, he was at the other end of the paternal scale, desperate for a child. She knew that he and his wife were undergoing fertility treatment, making her wonder if his objections were personal, whether convincing him would be her biggest challenge.

- 14 -

Clint arrived home to find just one light on in the kitchen and the rest of the apartment in darkness.

He called out, 'Hi, Gem. I'm home.' But there was no reply. Throwing his briefcase on the table, he flung back the shoji doors to the lounge to see Gemini lying on the sofa, her legs raised against an armrest. Her stomach looked enormous.

'Gem…Gem…' He shook her gently. 'Gem?'

Gemini stirred. 'Ummm. It's you, you're back, I must have dozed off.'

Clint released his breath slowly, not wanting her to know how irrationally worried he'd been.

'Can I get you something?' he asked.

Shaking her head, she sat up and told him about her day. How the doctor had told her to leave work early to give her time to rest before the twins were born.

Later in the evening, over dinner, they worked out the date she should finish work, and discussed car seats, cots and other baby essentials along with their plans for decorating the nursery.

'I know I don't say it often enough,' he said, drawing her protectively to him, 'but you're doing a fantastic job. I love you so much.'

Gemini's eyes filled with tears, and it made him feel guilty because he could tell she'd been missing his closeness; he'd been too preoccupied by work to give her the attention she deserved.

In the subdued lighting he saw the special effort she made with her make-up. He wondered if she'd been crying, and he sympathised with her, for while he was thriving on the thrill of his new job she was struggling with such vast physical changes. Emotionally it had to be hard on her; he knew that.

They held each other silently for a while. When Gemini spoke again she said, 'Do you remember our wedding vows - to have and to hold from this day forward...'

Clint joined in, 'For richer and poorer, in sickness and in health, till death us do part.'

'I was thinking that that is the level of commitment our babies will expect from us, the sort of commitment all parents should make to their children before they have them. Don't you think the world would be a better place if all prospective parents were asked to take those vows?'

'If only,' he said, loving the incorrigible romantic she was. He lowered his hand to stroke Gemini's stomach, and as he did so he felt some movement, perhaps a foot. In his mind he made a promise that he would always make his family the top priority in his life. He felt another kick, or was it a punch, and visualised a small hand in there.

When Katrina heard Stefano draw breath to speak she let out an exaggerated sigh and raised her eyes to the ceiling but, tempted though she was to storm impatiently from the room, she knew it was best to thrash out every last ounce of discussion rather than reconvene another day.

Taking control of herself, she scanned the room: Jackson was visibly ready to maim, not being the sort of man who should be detained in meetings too long. Brandon was still enjoying the debate, like a kitten jingling a ball with a bell inside he had a boyish enthusiasm for these sorts of encounters. And Stefano - she looked at him and mentally shook her head. While she liked him for not being a yes-man, there were times he was damned infuriating.

'I'm dead against it, I think it's irresponsible to go direct to the consumer. I don't believe the public have the knowledge they need to handle that sort of medical information wisely, there'll be all sorts of repercussions… '

'I think you underestimate the public,' intercepted Katrina. 'Other self-monitoring tests are available. Is ours much different to diagnostic tests like the pregnancy test, urine tests, blood sugar or cholesterol checks?'

'Of course we're different! With our test, lives are at stake.'

She pulled a face, faking surprise. 'And patients on the point of cardiac collapse or diabetic coma, their lives *aren't* at stake?'

'But that's not the point,' Stefano said grumpily. 'Patients need proper counseling. We have a responsibility to future generations to restrict its use otherwise Invivotest could be opening the door to population control policies based on all sorts of prejudices. I don't want to be sent to purgatory for my part in enabling neo-nazism.'

'Ha! That's way over the top.' Brandon let out a theatrical laugh and pretended to clap. 'Anyway, who's going to stop the doctors from playing God?'

Stefano squinted and gave Brandon a forced smile. Brandon returned the grin with slightly less menace because, unlike his older opponent, he was only arguing for sport.

Dwayne rallied behind Brandon. 'Half of them already think they're God,' he said. 'And I wonder how many with bulk-funding contracts will see this as a way to reduce future high-expense, high-needs patients.'

'I don't believe any of my colleagues would stoop that low,' Stefano growled.

Brandon laughed cynically. 'I wouldn't put it past some of those mercenary bastards,' he said.

Stefano's face flushed red and Clint interrupted. 'I'm more concerned about the ethical issues we're forcing these doctors to get involved in. A Catholic doctor is unlikely to suggest his patient does the test if it's going to lead to a termination, is he?'

Katrina quickly intervened to stop anyone else raising a hypothetical question. 'If we sell direct, only one person dictates what's moral and what's not. The customer. They either buy it or they don't. What could be simpler than that?'

Outside the siren of an ambulance could be heard squealing as it hurried past.

'I'm with you, Katrina,' Dwayne said. 'Let's get on with it.'

Katrina smiled inwardly; judging by that comment Dwayne was on her side. She wondered about Michael, he still hadn't said anything.

'What do you think, Michael?' she asked. All heads in the room turned.

He spoke slowly, a serious tone in his voice. 'I'm worried for the patients when they get their results. I think they need professional counseling, not just a printout through the mail.' Katrina frowned; she knew as well as everyone in the room that this man and his wife had suffered more intimate dealings with doctors than most people would in a lifetime. 'Imagine opening your mail and having to wait to see your doctor. At least if the doctor delivers the results they can discuss any medical options with the customer right away.'

'Hear, hear,' said Stefano, glad of an ally at last.

'You think the doctor will break it to them gently?' asked Dwayne, raising one eyebrow comically. 'That'll be the day!'

'Doctors are experts at handling that sort of information,' said Stefano sniffily. A few at the table sniggered.

Michael waited for the room to go to quiet. 'I'm also concerned about affordability. If it has to be paid for out of people's pockets there are going to be some who won't be able to afford it.'

'We'll be able to sell enough without having to worry about being reimbursed,' said Brandon, sounding like the eager accountant he was.

'Sales weren't my main concern,' Michael snapped.

'Tell us,' said Katrina, putting her hand up to stop Brandon interrupting again.

'This is a human rights issue, I don't want to see anybody excluded on the basis of cost,' Michael said.

Katrina nodded. 'But if it's reimbursable then your insurer, or employer, might feel they're entitled to see the results, and there'll be lots of opposition to that.' She dropped her tone as though she was talking to a frightened child. 'Think about your situation: would you want to get permission from your insurer as to whether or not you can have the baby?' A breathless silence hung over the table, all eyes fixed on a distant point somewhere in the room, anywhere so long as it wasn't directly on Katrina or Michael. This was personal ground she was treading on, and no one could predict how he might take it.

'Of course not,' he spat.

Bullseye! With a flutter of anticipation, Katrina realised they were ready to vote.

'All those in favor of marketing direct to the consumer raise your hand.' She waited, then counted. 'Six.'

'All those against?'

Stefano raised his hand, holding it high above his head. 'I'm not prepared to trade in *my* Hippocratic oath for dollars,' he said. 'This will never have my approval; it seems to me like you are setting sail with all the arrogance of the *Titanic*, 'Not even God can sink her' was what someone once said.'

- 15 -

Over the next four weeks Steen and Katrina spent many long hours in meetings completing the information required by the NASDAQ Securities and Exchange Commission. Clint was often called in to discuss the prospectus: its wording, design and graphics. This was what he loved - defining future possibilities, creating the promises of a new product, shaping a corporate persona.

Behind closed doors Katrina and Brandon played with spreadsheets of numbers. The decision to go direct to the consumer multiplied costs exponentially, and interest on the money alone could rapidly throw all their business plans into jeopardy if sales were slow to take off.

At one memorable meeting Brandon presented the management team with his five-year plan of the company's projected growth path. At the end of it Katrina got so excited she called for a celebration. Breaking into the wine reserves, Sarah brought out a bottle and a tray of champagne flutes, and thirty minutes later had some caterers deliver a sumptuous feast.

Swallowing a mouthful of caviar, Katrina touched Clint's arm. 'Look at those,' she said, her eyes directing him to the numbers scribbled on the whiteboard. 'Just look at the possibilities!'

Her hand rested on his arm and her fingers pinched him lightly. 'Yes,' he said, reluctantly, 'very exciting.'

'You know what, Clint,' she said, her eyes sparkling with champagne, 'it's the possibilities that inspire me.'

For some reason he felt an irrational urge to say: 'It's those possibilities that frighten me,' but instead, he forced a fake laugh, and though it didn't sound convincing she didn't seem to notice.

Until now he had never seen the extent of her lack of objectivity, and that worried him, because the more time he spent with her the more likely it was he would lose all sense of his own. Then he was offered another glass of wine, and joining the others in a toast to Invivotest, he dismissed his concerns - with four million babies born in America each year, the possibilities were awesome.

Eventually the celebration drew to a close and Clint and Dr Silvano were left alone in the room.

'Have you got a moment, Clint?' Stefano asked.

'Sure. What do you want?'

Stefano paused awkwardly. 'The thing is, Clint, I'll accept I've lost the battle on the distribution of Invivotest, and maybe it doesn't matter where the test is purchased, but it does matter how the customer gets their results, and how they interpret them. As a doctor I've seen how hard it is for people to accept information of this nature.'

Clint frowned. 'But you know we can't send the results to a doctor. The patient must be able to decide who has access to this information. Anyway, any woman who receives a difficult diagnosis will see her own doctor as a matter of course. The system is set up perfectly.'

'I don't agree, Clint, I think you've been bulldozed into Katrina's way of thinking. This whole issue needs to be given more thought.' Stefano paused, giving Clint the sort of look that suggested he was wondering if he should go on. Then he continued, his voice lower than before, 'I know you and Gemini haven't used Invivotest, I've always taken that as a sign you're not totally brainwashed by this organisation.'

Clint blanched. He wished Stefano hadn't used his personal situation as leverage because if it'd been up to him, he would've tested. In fact remembering back to when Gemini had made him promise not to use Invivotest, he'd felt as emotionally manipulated then, as he did now.

'Let me think me about it,' Clint said, not wanting to make any promises.

'Sometimes I think I'm in the wrong job,' Stefano said. 'Do you ever wonder if you're doing the right thing?'

'Sure. I'll bet everyone has doubts some days,' Clint said, trying to sound nonchalant, wishing he could forget Stefano's comments - but the truth was, as his babies' birth date drew closer, the uncertainty bothered him more and more.

Clint barely heard Stefano's reply. 'Mine's more than that. I have real misgivings.'

The following day Clint short-listed two advertising agencies from the six that had submitted credentials and strategic outlines. He phoned both companies telling them to present creative ideas for a television and print campaign and spent the rest of the day gathering together the data they'd need.

On Friday he met Stefano again. This time they kept strictly to business discussing the content of patient booklets and the 1-800 advice line, raising more questions than they had time to answer: How much information should the patient receive? Should the company employ qualified genetic counselors to answer the calls or could anyone be trained to read from a script? How could they reduce their ten-page disclaimer down to one?

In the weekend Clint, Katrina and Michael attended a biotechnology conference. Clint invited Gemini along, promising to spend some time with her.

Clint enjoyed the chance to catch up with old colleagues and hear the latest news and gossip until he heard the rumor that Zenogen had inside contacts fast-tracking their regulatory approval. Inuterogene might only have a three-month jump on them, nowhere near time enough to establish a niche. Zenogen obviously had friends in high places. Who was helping them short-circuit the legal process? What would their strategy be: doctor only or mass market? And what price? Even thinking about it was giving him a headache. It seemed so unfair Inuterogene would have to take all the risks, for such a small time advantage.

***

Gemini was reading a book when she heard the key turn in the lock.

Clint dropped his conference notes on top of the coffee table and went straight to the bathroom to find some pills and pour a glass of water.

'You're back early,' Gemini said, then she saw how pale he was. 'Are you sick?'

'I've got a headache,' Clint said, as he took off his shoes and got into bed fully clothed. 'I'm sorry, I can't talk, I've got to try and sleep it off.' He rolled over and kissed her. 'Can you wake me when it's time to go for dinner?'

Several minutes later he fell asleep, and Gemini read until her eyes glazed over and she dozed off, her book falling to the floor.

When Gemini woke the red numbers on the clock display blinked 7:15 and for a moment she wasn't sure if it was morning or night. The space beside her was empty and the bedclothes smoothed up. Calling out, the bathroom sounded hollow and empty and when she looked in the wardrobe she saw Clint's dinner jacket was gone.

He hadn't bothered to wake her! Gemini snatched a shopping bag off the floor and pulled out a black evening gown. She grabbed the price tag in one hand and felt a satisfying rip as the washing instructions tore in half. He hadn't wanted her to come this weekend - she rolled her leggings down and in long vicious stomps fought her way out of them - he thought she was a nuisance, an interruption to his precious work.

She threw the dress on, her hair bristling with static as the fabric fell around her in cool voluptuous sheens. Then she saw herself in the mirror and laughed at her disheveled hair, some loose ends sticking out from the electricity.

Steadying her hand she applied her makeup, and fiddled with her hair, calming her mind, then she practiced her smile in the mirror - all part of her plan to play the corporate wife - that clearly was what Clint really wanted.

The last few guests were being shown to their tables when Gemini arrived at the ballroom. Gemini took her seat and listened to the president's welcoming speech, the atmosphere in the room effervescing excitement and optimism. At this conference they were going to hear about the future possibilities of medicine, they were going to end pain and suffering, revolutionise healthcare, turn water into wine.

During the applause Gemini saw Katrina whispering in Clint's ear, he looked happy, his headache presumably gone. Turning to Michael instead she joked that perhaps they should all stand and say *Amen* but Michael didn't laugh, and she made another mental note to keep her opinions to herself. While they waited for their meals Gemini listened politely as Michael told her about his future plans for Invivotest until he became too technical and she simply nodded her head.

Later he asked Gemini about her pregnancy before discussing the fertility treatments he and his wife were undergoing. Explaining the process, in more detail than she wanted to know, she sensed uncertainty in his voice, fear that his beloved science might fail to deliver. Then he told her about the protestors who threatened to stop the clinic performing this controversial new procedure and her sympathy soured as she realised it wasn't science's failure he feared, but the restraint of its power.

At nine o'clock the lights were dimmed and the speeches began. Gemini tried to not cringe visibly every time someone mentioned the word 'benefits' - benefits to whom? Who decides quality of life? What do *they* know about a divine plan?

When the speeches finally ended, a band started to play and Gemini used her pregnancy as an excuse to leave for an early night, and though she could tell Clint would have liked to stay longer, he joined her.

Alone in their room, Clint took Gemini in his arms and thanked her for her patience. 'It must have been really boring for you,' he said in a whisper as he undressed her, caressed her shoulders, her back, her front, and their babies. Later, when he made love to her, his lips tenderly brushing her ears, Gemini felt only subdued elation when he told her in short bursts how much he loved her: truly, passionately, madly, deeply.

Jackson took a bite of his chicken penang and tried to block his nose to the smell of urine that steamed from the open gutter behind. Lifting one hand to wipe some sauce from his mouth he caught a whiff of his own underarm odor, he felt off-color, but then he never felt particularly well when he was away on trips like this.

This morning he'd been unable to find an international telephone connection that worked. Apparently the Xhiang-Lioa exchange was down though the operators had given him different stories in broken English each time. The first excuse involved a flash flood and he was told the technicians would have the exchange working by lunchtime. At midday he was told there'd been a fire and the phone lines were being diverted, and if he called back at two p.m. they would definitely be able to put him through. At two he was told the exchange was out of action for another few hours and all communication would be impossible. 'This is not America you know, sir,' he'd been told with mocking insincerity.

After three days of this stinking place he decided he'd been jerked around enough; he wanted a drink, preferably tequila with a slice of lemon and lots of salt. On this trip he'd had difficulty extracting information, and he wouldn't have waited this long except he'd dealt with this company before and their reliability and quality control had been excellent back then.

Thinking about it now, the secrecy was unprecedented - for a few American dollars he normally could find out anything he required - it had to be Zenogen: somehow they'd stitched up a deal good enough to cut Inuterogene out of the picture.

Someone rubbed against his elbow and he shifted on his stool to move over a fraction. Turning to look at his new neighbor he saw she was beautiful, and making herself available. For a little bit more than the price of a bowl of egg noodles he thought she'd be well worth it. He gave the girl his hotel room number and told her to meet him there at 4.30 p.m. In the meantime he set out to change his tickets, he'd catch a plane to Tokyo and give head office a call from there.

Katrina wore a dark blue suit with gold triangular buttons and a long gold chain around her neck. Her hair had just been restyled and trimmed to shoulder length, and was streaked with pink-blonde highlights that offset her blue eyes.

She opened the meeting with the news that Jackson was now in Tokyo negotiating with an alternative supplier. Refusing to indulge in any speculation she deftly moved the discussion onto other matters.

'Clint, do you want to give us an update on your activities?'

Clint took the floor, announcing his plans to appoint a sales manager and two new sales teams - one team to sell directly to doctors, and the other to take orders from retailers while also doing in-store and window displays. Next he told the meeting they could expect to receive their first copies of the company prospectus off the press later that week, a cheer went up around the room.

'And now,' he said, 'the news you've all been waiting for - our first ever media event is scheduled for Friday the fifteenth.' He put his hands in the air and pretended to play a trumpet. 'Ta-da-da-taa!'

Brandon clapped, and Clint gave him a mock bow before adopting a more serious look and tone. 'The press invites are going out in tomorrow's mail. I have prepared a media kit,' he said, holding it up for all to see. 'Sarah will give you each a copy on your way out. Between now and then I've arranged for a specialist course in public relations for Katrina as she's not going to win this battle on the strength of her good looks alone.'

He smiled at Katrina and looked around the room while the others gave her some non-verbal encouragement. 'We'll be building up Katrina's scientific reputation although we don't want to do too good a job and make her look like a pie-in-the-sky scientist who's out of touch with reality. She'll be working hard to adopt the right sort of look that'll score us lots of good publicity.'

Clint paused. 'I think you all understand our need to balance the amount of press we get. We want enough to get interest from investors willing to contribute to our balance sheet, but not so much that we create any controversy in the Senate - although I think it's safe to assume they won't want to intervene, our industry is worth too much to them.'

Over the next few days Katrina practiced speaking to different camera angles. 'The language you use is very important,' said Jeana, the image consultant. 'Remember in Vietnam they didn't shoot people, they shot geeks. Countries don't go to war anymore, they go on peace-making missions, I know its semantics but the words you use are vitally important. And be careful of product placement, where you stand and by whom. You'll find you need eyes in the back of your head, but you don't want to appear on national television with a 'Ban all testing' placard behind you. If you're not sure what to say, repeat the question - or repeat what you just said if it was worth repeating.'

'Repeat what you just said?' Katrina joked.

'You've got it!' said Jeana, waving five perfectly manicured fingers in Katrina's direction. 'And never be afraid to pause for dramatic effect. Speak slowly. Turn your head this way and never move too quickly for the camera. Don't wear too much jewelry. Under no circumstances lie. You might have to be circumspect with the truth, but always remember Bill Clinton and that woman. And remember, if you're really stuck answer a question with another question, it's the oldest trick in the book.'

'So you think I should answer a question with a question?'

Jeana gave Katrina the thumbs up. 'School's out.'

Katrina stood and headed towards the door - the scientist in her had had more than enough of Ms Verte and her false eyelashes, fake laugh and reflective personality.

- 16 -

Katrina arrived at the Sheraton Plaza two hours before the media conference was due to start. Soon after she'd introduced herself to Tara, the event organiser, she was told there was a man waiting in the conference room for her. Opening the doors, Katrina stepped inside expecting to see Clint who'd agreed to meet her at the venue. Instead, her face froze as a stranger rose from his chair and started walking towards her.

It was his stature, the strength and flowing grace of his purposeful stride that she recognised first. Scott Braxton.

In what seemed like her next conscious moment Katrina discovered he was standing in front of her, reaching out to shake her hand. Then she heard him say, 'It *is* you!'

She dropped her hand, her mind lost in an abyss of time. No amount of practice sessions with image consultants could have prepared her for this.

'It's great to see you,' he said, his soft brown eyes exploring hers.

She took in his face; the same fine lines she remembered creasing into familiar grooves, only deeper now. Though she dropped her gaze, she could still feel his attention, curiosity amplified after all these years.

'You all right, M'am?' Tara asked.

Katrina nodded mutely.

'We're buddies,' Scott said, 'from a long time ago. Here, let me help you with your gear.'

Katrina passed him her laptop still struggling to think of something to say until finally it seemed so much time had gone by, anything would do.

'What are you doing here?' she said, surprised her voice worked at all.

Tara pointed to the badge on Scott's lapel, and gave a broad grin. 'He's the boss!' she said.

Katrina smiled blankly; last she knew he'd won a swimming scholarship and was going to study law.

'You can go now, Tara,' Scott said, 'I'm happy to take care of Dr Dudek.'

Katrina waited for Tara to leave.

'Let me show you how everything works,' he said, taking her around the room, checking the location of light switches, microphones and power points.

'Is there anything else, I can get you?'

'No thanks. I think I've got all I need.'

'In that case, I guess I'd better leave you time to prepare,' he said, starting to move, reluctantly it seemed, towards the door.

'There's just one thing,' Katrina said, 'I was wondering when this is over, if you'd like to catch up over coffee - perhaps sometime later next week?'

'I'd like that,' Scott said, pulling a card from his suit pocket. 'You know where to find me but here's my number just in case.'

She took the card from him.

'Good luck with your meeting,' he said, then in one quick movement, he leant forward and kissed her on the cheek. A shiver ran down her spine, and for a long time after she felt the lingering touch of his lips where they'd brushed her skin.

Katrina signaled Clint to motion the unruly clutter of voices to be quiet. He welcomed their guests and gave his introductory speech before taking a seat at the back of the room. Alone on the podium, afire with nervous anticipation, Katrina took her first question from a reporter sitting in the front row.

'Can you determine sex?' asked the young man from *American News*.

'Yes,' Katrina replied, resisting the urge to say more, planning to keep her answers succinct as Jeana had told her to.

'What's to stop people terminating babies on the basis of gender?'

'Nothing,' Katrina said, 'except we won't disclose that information.'

'Your question?' she said, pointing to a woman from *Medical News*.

'What's the reliability of the test? And is there a risk of false positives?' the reporter asked.

'The genetic probes are 100% reliable so there can be no false positives on the three hundred and fifty-six chromosomal and genetic abnormalities we can currently test…And with advances in our knowledge of the human genome that list will continue to grow.'

'There are degrees of Down Syndrome. Can you test for the severity it?'

'No,' Katrina answered.

'How much will these tests cost?' asked the reporter from *World*.

'We're aiming for around the one-hundred-dollar mark, or a little less. We want it to be affordable to the average American consumer,' she said, smiling warmly. Positive coverage in that publication would have credibility with doctors and investors alike.

'Will insurers have access to the results of these tests?'

'We'll be sending the results back to the consumer. Whether they pass this information on to their insurer is up to them.'

Katrina pointed at an attractive young woman in a wheelchair representing a magazine called *Tomorrow's Challenge*.

'Some rare disorders already have a problem finding funding for new treatments and cures. Surely this test will reduce the number of children born with those diseases - then who will bother doing the research?'

All background noise in the room stopped, and Katrina could feel the anticipation of her audience waiting like predators, even though the question was unfair.

'The funding of research has always been determined by market forces,' Katrina said, slowing her reply, wondering how much controversy she dared. 'In fact, when you think about it, we're offering an alternative cure.'

Voices rallied everywhere. Katrina's attention was drawn to the loudest - a woman in a university sweatshirt with blue streaks in her long black hair. 'But what about the rights of the unborn child?' she yelled, her tongue stud clearly visible from the stage. 'Don't those with genetic disabilities have the right to be born?'

Raising her voice to be heard above the noise, Katrina responded quickly, small beads of sweat formed on her upper lip. 'Perhaps you could find a way to get their consent,' she said, pausing, feeling the adrenalin pumping. 'And when you do, we'll ask them for it, okay?'

Some laughter, boos, shouts ricocheted all around.

Clint walked from the back of the room. 'One at time. Quiet, please,' he said repeatedly until order was restored. 'We've only got time for a couple more questions.'

The uproar gave Katrina time to survey the room. Eventually she pointed to a conservative-looking woman who wore a business-like red jacket and stood to ask her question. 'Will Inuterogene be taking out shares in abortion clinics?'

'Absolutely not,' Katrina said. 'We are providers of a diagnostic tool. We are not a medical clinic.'

'But what about the politics of the Invivotest?' the woman persisted. 'What will happen if they discover a gene for paedophilia, will you release that information when it comes to hand?'

'We'll cross that bridge when we get to it,' Katrina said, shaking her head, visibly trying to discredit the idea, knowing it to be a gray area. Who knew where gene mapping could lead? What if there was a clairvoyant gene? A mental illness gene, or one for aggression, happiness, criminality?

Wanting to change the subject she searched the room for the quiet looking reporter she'd seen earlier; someone she thought would ask something innocuous.

'What view does Inuterogene take on genetic mutations - are they a natural way for the species to adapt?' he asked, holding his microphone forwards.

With despair, Katrina read its label: *The Green Planet*.

'They may be,' she replied cautiously.

'Over time, wouldn't the widespread use of Invivotest cull out some of these handicaps, and mightn't we then be interfering with the natural evolution of mankind?'

'The evolution of mankind?' she said, smiling broadly, trying to make light of him, aware of a television camera crew moving forwards into a space nearer the front. 'I don't think that's something I feel qualified to comment on,' she said. 'Besides, you could argue antibiotics, vaccines and any life-saving drugs also have a similar effect.'

Catching some movement out of the corner of her eyes, Katrina turned to see the woman with the red jacket leaping up from her chair. 'But the Invivotest isn't life-saving, is it?' she yelled.

Remembering she was being filmed, Katrina fixed her face with a smile.

- 17 -

Katrina slouched in the car seat beside Clint; she'd hardly spoken since the press function ended. All things considered, Clint thought it had gone quite well - there was bound to be some controversy.

Sitting up, Katrina raked a hand through her hair and shook her head from side to side as though she was trying to wake herself up. 'Why do people assume unplanned populations are better than planned populations?' she asked.

Clint lifted his hands off the steering wheel and gave an exaggerated shrug. 'Dunno,' he said, his eyes fixed on the road in front. 'Apart from a few of the greenies, I doubt most people ever gave it much thought.'

'Exactly!' said Katrina. 'In reality people determine the future gene pool when they choose their partner…And I'll bet a lot of the people who think fetal testing affects the natural order of the gene pool conveniently forget when they use a condom they're interfering with nature's population planning.'

Clint pondered this. 'I guess it's a hangover from religious beliefs. Like a lot of things,' he said. 'Like it's holy to suffer. Did you notice how all the journos seemed to be so anti-technology? Even the women's groups were negative. I would've thought they'd be pleased that we're giving women more choice over the outcome of their pregnancy.'

A car swerved in front of them and then back to the inside lane.

'He must be drunk, or on something,' Clint said, putting his fist on the horn and leaving it there for a five-second blast. The other driver gave them the fingers in the rear-vision mirror and Clint cursed under his breath.

'People like that should be lined up against a wall and shot,' he said. 'No, that's too easy. They should be castrated with a blunt pocket knife and a piece of string.' He laughed to let her know he was joking.

Stopping for coffee, looking conspicuously over-dressed, they took a table at the rear of The Hungry Mule and ordered their food. When the waitress left, Katrina continued. 'What annoys me is that we have restraints on our conduct everywhere else. We conform to certain rules by the way we act towards one another, the way we drive our cars, pay our taxes - but any fool can have a baby. Yet a couple's decision to have a child affects us all. Society still has to provide facilities to accommodate one more - so why can't we have a say in what type of children we want brought into this world?'

Clint groaned and looked over his shoulder to check no one was listening. 'I hope this place isn't bugged. I can see the headlines now: Welcome to Katrina Dudek's brave new world.'

Katrina grinned. 'You might disapprove but society should think about these things especially with the genetic technologies coming through now. A new age of reproductive policies isn't so far-fetched. Seriously, Clint, why is our right to reproduce so fiercely defended when I can't even walk down the street naked without getting arrested?'

Clint started to reply, but before he had chance Katrina added, 'And don't give me that right-to-life stuff. Economists already decide rights to life when they allow a premature baby to gobble up millions of taxpayers' dollars while refusing to fund a coronary by-pass operation…So, why Clint, why do we allow people the right to breed indiscriminately?'

Clint saw the waitress approaching and pursed his lips to tell Katrina to 'Ssshhh'.

'And what about my rights to freedom of speech?' she asked.

'You sold those a long time ago!' he said, and they both laughed.

Katrina leant back in her chair to give their waitress enough room to slam two huge plates of nachos in front of them. The shock of the impact caused a landslide on Clint's corn chip mountain and the three watched the sour cream peak topple over, pulling a slurry of melted cheese and guacamole in its wake, finally stopping in a pile in the middle of the table.

Clint kept his face deadpan and held his mobile phone out towards the waitress. 'Do you want to call 911 or should I?'

They all laughed then the waitress moved them to a different table, bringing them another serving. Clint helped himself to a chip.

'Why is everyone so quick to put the rights of the unborn ahead of the mother?' Katrina asked. 'It's not as though they'll be there to wipe the baby's bottom. They're not the ones who'll have to worry who's going to care for their still-dependent adult-child once they're gone.'

Something in her tone reminded Clint of the night Gemini and Katrina first met. He recalled their discussion those last few moments as they stood by the door: *was* the decision to have a child one of the head or the heart? Two such different approaches to life yet still he couldn't decide.

'And it seems so hypocritical,' Katrina said, 'for our motives to be attacked when women are getting pregnant everyday with less effort and thought than it takes to learn how to drive a car. It doesn't seem right a baby can be born with such scant regard.'

Clint paused; it'd almost sounded as if there was something personal in what she was saying - surely she'd never wanted children of her own?

They ate the rest of their food and drank their coffee, and when they stood to leave Clint left the waitress a generous tip.

On her last day at work Gemini had meant to give a speech but her words got all muddled. Blame it on your hormones her work colleagues had kindly said before giving her a farewell present - two teddy bears sitting in highchairs.

That evening Gemini waited for Clint to get home, desperate for someone to talk to. It had only just struck her that day how much being a mother would change her identity and there was no way of getting out of it now.

Gemini rushed to Clint as soon as he got in the door. He hugged her, running his hand across her stomach. 'How are my babies doing in there?' he said.

'Fine,' she said, wishing he'd asked about her personally and not just the twins. 'They've taken up Morris dancing, my skin's going to be so stretched you'll be able to park the car in there when they're done.'

Later that evening they sat on the balcony watching the sun go down, discussing the practicalities of having twins. Gemini told him that her mother had volunteered to come and help out for a few weeks after the birth.

'Do you want her to?' Clint asked diplomatically.

'I'm not sure; I didn't want to hurt her feelings so I told her I'd check with you.'

'Well, I can hardly say no, can I?' Clint said.

'Not really,' Gemini said. 'But looking on the bright side, I guess she knows how to deal with twins, she coped with me and Hudson, after all.'

'And that was some achievement too, I'll bet!' said Clint with a laugh.

That night Gemini tried to sleep, but the babies seemed to have saved all their energies for an indoor football tournament. Turning onto her side, then onto her back, she arranged pillows behind her, between her legs, around her belly, but nothing seemed comfortable. In the end she got out of bed and ran a bath.

As she lay in the warm water she watched the contortions under her belly and wondered if she'd be able to deliver naturally? How had it been for her birth mother?

The thoughts brought with them a familiar unease: Why had her mother had her? Had she been raped? Was she religious? Or had she been too young and unable to afford them? Or had she no choice at all, unable to find an abortionist in time?

Gemini pulled the plug and stood to dry herself. Her stretched belly filled the mirror and guiltily she thought about Pamela, her adoptive mother, an infertile role model, but still the person she owed so much.

Getting back into bed she felt a violent kick that made her wince in the dark. Rubbing her belly firmly, she willed the foot to move inside.

Clint moaned and turned over, taking half the sheets with him, and she held her breath, wondering if she'd woken him or if he'd sensed what she was thinking. She had so many questions she would like answered but last time they'd discussed this, he'd asked her what she'd do if she found her birth mother was an alcoholic, sick or demented - would she want to get involved then? Would she feel like she had to? How could it not turn into a question of who owed what to whom?

Reluctantly Gemini knew he was right, but it was hard to dismiss her mythical past. As a four-year-old she'd dreamt her mother was a beautiful gypsy, her father a handsome prince, not a bit like Pamela and John. At seven she was the lovechild of a glamorous Hollywood actress with delicious fantasies of her mother coming to reclaim her. Only adopted children could be 'found' and believing that had made her special.

At ten the fantasies were more mundane - any woman could be her mother. Women at the bus stop, pushing supermarket trolleys or driving cars that turned the same corners taking the same route home, following her, checking she was all right. And with sexual awareness came more possibilities - the lady down the street who'd had her illegitimately - and for a while she entertained the thought she was her father's daughter all along, born to another woman but adopted by Pamela to escape the shame.

Now, at twenty-four years old, awake in the early hours of the morning, the fantasy was disappointingly ordinary. Her birth mother was probably happily married with two children and a cocker spaniel and would resent the knock on the door. Clint was right. *Forget it girl, get some sleep.*

Part Three

- 18 -

For weeks now, Gemini hadn't had a decent night's sleep, her mind drifting, always waking feeling somehow incomplete.

But tonight something felt different. The bedside clock blinked 2:02 a.m. Gemini sat up in bed and felt a contraction clutch her stomach into a tight vice-like ache. Breathing out slowly through pursed lips, she got out of bed and went to pack her toothbrush and other last-minute essentials into the bag she'd prepared weeks ago.

She looked at Clint sleeping peacefully and felt a rush of tenderness for him. If only she always felt this way about him, but lately he'd been so preoccupied with work she'd felt repulsed. She knew he was trying to do his best for her - by providing for her - but it was his love and closeness she really wanted.

Ahhh! She clasped her stomach and checked her watch. The contractions were getting harder, about ten minutes apart. She decided to wake Clint, then called the doctor who agreed to meet them at the hospital in half an hour.

Outside it was hot and some drizzle fell onto the windscreen, leaving elongated reflections of the yellow and white streetlights. Neither said much. Clint concentrated on his driving and Gemini saved her breath, the hum of the air-conditioning and the hypnotic shh-lop of the windscreen wipers filling the quietness.

By the time they got to the hospital Gemini was glad she hadn't left it any longer; the contractions were coming more rapidly, each seeming to lift, squeeze, ache and crush all at once. The nurse helped her onto a bed. 'How much more of this will I have to put up with?' Gemini asked, frightened of the pain. 'Oohhh…here comes another. Where's the anesthesiologist? Please tell him to hurry up.'

'Breathe!' commanded the nurse, cutting through Gemini's panic. 'You can do it.'

Clint rubbed Gemini's back until she told him it was irritating her so he went and sat in a chair. The nurse pulled a trolley towards the bed and attached three belts around Gemini's waist - one for each babies heartbeat and one for the contractions. Turning the fetal heart monitor on, the machine's black ink laser mirrored the intensity of the contractions, establishing a pattern of the babies' heartbeats. A duet of rapid chuf-chuf-chuf-chuf noises echoed around the room.

Dr Stone paged the anesthesiologist, and had just finished examining Gemini when she felt a never-ending warm flooding around her legs. 'Your waters have broken,' he said dispassionately. 'That'll hurry things up.'

With the intensity of the next contraction Gemini lost all control, screaming, feeling the full extent of her fear. After what seemed like hours, but was according to the clock only five and a bit minutes, the anesthesiologist hurried in and set about inserting an epidural needle.

After a while Gemini felt a cold trickle down her spine, and with relief she noticed each contraction seemed to get weaker until she could see the jagged lines of each contraction on the monitor, but barely feel them.

Further down the ward she could hear the low groans of another woman in labor, the moaning getting louder, lower, and more frequent, followed by sudden quietness. All senses primed, she expected to hear the sound of rushing feet, but then a shrill newborn's scream broke the silence. Tears filled her eyes. 'Its first breath,' Gemini said, her voice trembling in awe of the enormity of that moment.

Again the ward seemed to hum and whir like it had before. To the sound of the twins' heartbeats, Gemini closed her eyes to nap, the epidural dissolving her pain. Clint dozed off in a reclining chair beside the bed.

Half asleep, her mind still floating in a type of semi-consciousness, Gemini was aware a nurse came in, lifting her arm to take her blood pressure. Somewhere far away she could hear the urgent ping-ping-ping of an electronic alarm that grew louder, until she awakened fully to see her doctor staring intently at the fetal heart monitor.

One of the black ink lines had dropped dramatically downwards. With brutal force, the doctor prodded his fingers into her belly and then around her crotch, feeling for the baby's position. Pulling his hand away abruptly, he took three long steps to the doors and pulled them both open, calling to the nurses down the hallway, 'Theatre. Quick.' In his voice Gemini heard a calm that was too controlled and she felt a sickening fear clamp her heart.

In a frantic flurry of activity the fetal heart monitor belts were unstrapped, the brakes on the bed released and the bed rushed down the corridor, jerking to a halt under the circular theatre lights.

'We'll need an epidural top up, page Dr Watts,' the obstetrician commanded. 'Nurse, get Mr. Harrison a gown. What pediatrician's on tonight? Try Dr Singh.'

Within minutes Dr Stone was scrubbed up, waiting for the anesthesiologist to give him the nod. Clint stood near Gemini's head. 'Don't worry, you'll be fine, the babies will be fine,' he murmured, more often than necessary.

Gemini's heart pounded; this was nothing like she'd expected. She could feel some tapping and banging and fumbling as the scalpel sliced into her womb, the numbness around her middle making her feel she couldn't breathe and she longed for the reassurance of the chuf-chuf-chuf of the fetal heart monitors.

Staring up at Clint she tried to interpret from the movement of his eyes what was happening on the other side of the screen. His eyes, framed within the surgical mask, darted from her face to the operation the other side of the screen, and at one point he squeezed his eyes shut and she guessed that he'd seen them pull back the skin on her stomach.

After that Clint kept his eyes firmly fixed on the obstetrician. Powerless to speak, Gemini's ears were tuned for every sound: the echo of a latex glove as it snapped into place, the drum of water against an aluminum sink, the rip of sterile packaging, the sound of surgical instruments as they rattled in a stainless steel dish. Every now and again someone on the medical team would say something reassuring, as though there was an unwritten code for time intervals between silences.

Gemini heard the room go quiet in a collective breath-hold; all eyes were fixed on what she presumed was one of her babies. The muscles in Clint's neck bulged as he swallowed hard, and then his pupils widened and she knew in that instant her first baby was born.

Straining to hear, Gemini heard Dr Stone mumble. 'Easy. Easy. Have you got him?' After a pause and some fumbling, she heard a 'yes', and she saw a floppy baby dangled overhead, its skin a bloodless white with a tinge of blue marbling.

Shocked, she lay like a deaf-mute, hearing only a boom - the absence of sound, ringing in her ears. Her ears at bursting point, she heard the snip of scissors and more footsteps as the pediatrician carried her baby to the far side of the room. Moving her head as far as she could, she saw a nurse flap a disposable sheet onto the bench, and the pediatrician place the baby on top.

She watched the changing outline of the doctor's back, shoulders and arms as he tended to her baby who lay motionless, his skin turning blue all over.

Aghast, she listened to the sounds of cupped hands tapping flesh and the vacuuming hiss of the suction, then a gurgling noise. Someone cheered and the doctor turned towards her and she heard her baby give it first quivering cry. Never before in her life had she felt so much relief, and infinite joy.

For the first time in ages Gemini became aware of Clint's presence. He eased his grip on her hand and she wriggled her fingers to get the circulation going. She half-laughed and half-cried as she caught sight of the tears that streamed down his face, but he didn't seem to notice, his eyes fixed on the operation behind the screen. Only when she felt Clint increase his grip again did she know she wouldn't have much longer to wait. Seconds later she saw the doctor raise his upper arms, lifting a baby high in the air for her to see and

Gemini wept with happiness, knowing the little girl's heart beat strongly on its own.

They'd been joking about names for a while and Clint had just suggested they call them Hannibal and Annabel so on a windy day it would sound like both names at once.

'I think we should call her Brianna. And this dear little boy here, I want his name to give him strength. What about Orion?' Gemini said, knowing, as far as she was concerned, his name was already decided.

Clint looked serious. It was at times like these she could see how different they were. He'd be thinking how their names would look on a school report or a business card while she'd be wondering about their numerological significance. In the silence she could almost see his cerebral cortex processing names as if children were new products to be launched.

Reading her mind, he said, 'Oh, I don't know. I'll have to run those names past the patent attorneys first.'

'Cl-i-nt.'

'I can live with Orion, but I'm not sure about Brianna. I think she's more like a...' He paused, keeping her in suspense, 'I think she's more like a Flame.'

Gemini's heart jumped. 'Flame! Clint, that's gorgeous, I *love* it!'

'Good, I'll be able to tell your mother when I pick her up,' he said.

'You'd better not be late,' Gemini said, knowing how much her mother would complain.

Clint kissed her goodbye, promising to return later. 'And you two give your mom a rest,' he said to Flame and Orion who were sleeping peacefully in their bassinet.

Clint swung into one of the airport's vacant parking bays, immediately catching sight of Gemini's mother sitting alone on a wooden bench surrounded by luggage. He knew the short flight would've been a major expedition for her but the distance that separated them had certain advantages, at least he didn't have to see her too often. They'd always got along on the surface but he'd always found her so uptight he couldn't relax when she was around.

He waved out to her as he approached and she waved back with such an embarrassing air-traffic-control movement he was glad when she'd stopped. Walking towards her he felt the closing distance intimidating; never knowing quite how to greet her, a hug being too intimate and a handshake too formal. Almost at the bench he was relieved to see Pamela had begun to sort her bags - luggage was something they both knew how to handle.

- 19 -

On the drive to Townsville, Katrina's feelings alternated from nervous to blasé then back to nervous again. She'd arranged to meet Scott at his place and now the time had come, she was having second thoughts: Why not leave bygones alone; why risk dragging up the past?

She found the street easily and pulled up outside number twenty-eight. The two-story villa was exactly how he'd described it, 'a little run down and a little done up' with a new coat of white paint and a shabby steel roof. She climbed the iron staircase, onto the creaky wooden verandah cluttered with some weed-filled flower pots and a falling-apart sofa covered by a rug matted with dog hairs.

Rapping the brass knocker, a dog barked enthusiastically and she could hear its paws scratching the wood. When the door opened she saw the tip of a black nose sniffing around the corner, then a hairy black and gray dog with cataracts over both eyes, slithered towards her. She bent forward to stroke him and he dropped on the floor, licking her toes.

Scott grabbed the dog's collar from behind and pulled him away. 'Move aside, Minstrel. Let the lady through, okay?'

Unhappy in his restraint, Minstrel gave her a dejected look and then slunk over to the sofa and slowly climbed aboard, sinking his face onto his outstretched paws.

'We'll leave him to it, shall we?' said Scott, ushering Katrina inside.

Katrina's eyes took a while to adjust to the dingy interior darkened by wooden floorboards and paneling that went halfway up the walls. The house reeked of paint and varnish fumes, and some brushes, trays and tools lay on the newspaper that covered the floor.

'Go on through to the kitchen,' Scott said, gesturing to the shaft of light that fanned through the doorway at the end of the hallway. 'At this time of the day most of the sun comes in the back of the house.'

Katrina chose a high stool at the breakfast bar, pulling off some newspaper that had stuck to the soles of her shoes.

'I'm in the middle of home renovations,' he said.

Katrina smiled at the obviousness of his remark.

'Just in case you thought I normally live like this,' he added.

Another unnecessary comment, she thought, a sure sign of nervousness. Offering to make them coffee, Katrina watched as he noisily emptied the dishwasher in search of a couple of clean mugs. She noticed the oven and marble bench-top all looked new. Random streaks of white paint on the glass in the main windows drew attention to the newly painted frames.

Feeling overpowered by the smell of paint fumes, garlic and cooking odors, Katrina swung herself down off her stool. 'I'll open a window, shall I?' she said.

'They're jammed shut with paint,' said Scott. 'Try that door there if you like.' He nodded towards a white-paneled door that was split in half like a stable door.

She slid the bolt, pushed the top half open and gasped. 'Wow, I had no idea you could see the sea from here.'

Unlatching the lower door, she stepped onto the tiny balcony, marveling at the sea of rooftops that sloped before her in a magnificent cityscape that stretched miles into the distance before blending with the harbor beyond. Leaning back against the railing, she enjoyed the mild breeze and sunshine on her face.

Scott joined her, squeezing alongside. 'There's barely room for two,' he said. 'One day I'll put a long window in this wall here to make the most of the view.' He raised his arm to indicate its position on the soon-to-be-remodeled wall.

Katrina turned in the direction he was pointing, wondering if he felt the same intimacy in their closeness, seeing nothing to suggest he did.

Overhead a seagull cawed and another gull swooped past. Wings outstretched, the pair circled in graceful arcs against the cloudless skies before flying around the side of the house and out of sight.

'I enjoy home renovations,' Scott said, breaking the silence. 'Would you like a guided tour?'

Katrina gratefully accepted. The villa was small: two bedrooms; a bathroom with a doorway that opened onto a sliver of a laundry; a dingy lounge with the original fireplace and 1920s stained-glass window; and a study lined with bookshelves that overshadowed a desk with a computer and printer on it.

Returning to the kitchen, she noticed a clock with a small metal airplane circling its face as it ticked the seconds away; it reminded her of the love-me, love-me-not clock, the first time she'd thought of that for over twenty years.

'The clock,' she said. 'Did you make it?'

'Yes,' he replied. 'Metalwork used to be a favorite hobby of mine.'

He'd said it as if she was a stranger, and she wondered if he remembered as much of the past as she did.

'Used to be?' she asked.

'I don't have a workshop here although I do keep meaning to go to night classes.'

Scott offered to make another coffee, which she accepted, sensing he found it easier to talk while doing something. Anything would do, even an activity as mundane as rinsing a coffee cup.

He turned off the tap. 'Are you married?' she asked.

'Divorced. She left me for a friend of mine. How about you?' He dried the mugs and placed them on the bench.

'Never married,' she said. 'No-one serious. I guess my career has always been my first love, my baby.' She hesitated then asked him if he had any children.

'No.' He opened the fridge and reached for the milk then closed the door. A photograph slipped onto the floor. 'They're my nieces and nephews, I have sixteen all told - four Catholic sisters, remember?'

She nodded. Mary, Janie, Gillian and Holly. She could remember their faces clearly.

'After the divorce came through and we'd settled the house, Patti told me she'd had a termination only a month after she left me. She knew I'd always wanted children…' His voice trailed off, she could feel his sadness and longing. 'What about you - did you have any more?'

'Who, me? No.' She shook her head, her mind working quickly. How had he found out, she'd been pregnant back then? No one was supposed to have known. Flustered, she said without thinking, 'They were twins.'

'Twins?'

She heard the shock register in his voice and realised then that what she'd stated as a fact, was confirmation too.

'I didn't keep them,' she said, fighting the impulse to run to her car, knowing there was nothing she could do to withdraw her words. She watched Scott, with his back to her, searching in a drawer for a teaspoon, seeming to take forever, surely it wasn't that hard to find one?

She fumbled for the right words to fill the chasm. 'Well, you know, babies never were high on my list of priorities, I wouldn't have made a good mother. Anyway, I was too young.' It sounded like a list of excuses when it'd been her choice all along.

Scott stood, motionless; no doubt he was thinking the babies were his.

'I had to study, I wanted to get established first,' she said, talking for the sake of it, wondering what he was feeling now she'd opened a whole new chapter in his life.

Finding a teaspoon he turned and placed the cups and sugar bowl in front of her.

'I wish I'd known,' he said.

'But we were so young,' Katrina said. 'Babies take away your freedom…They cost so much to keep… Aren't you glad I saved you from all that?'

Scott shrugged, and stared into his coffee mug. She wondered if she should tell him he may not be the father but it all seemed too much too soon.

Katrina finished her drink and stood to leave; this'd been a mistake, she shouldn't have come.

'Are you going already?' He seemed surprised. 'I was kinda hoping you'd have time for a walk with Minstrel and me.'

'Oh, I do,' she said. 'I wasn't sure you wanted me to stay.' She put her car keys back in her purse. 'I'd love to come.'

They locked the villa and went downstairs, heading towards the park. Minstrel scuttled in front, then stopped and turned, his shaggy body several times blocking their path.

'Mind out, you old fool,' Scott said, each time he had to push the dog out their way.

'What happened to the swimming?' Katrina eventually asked.

'Nothing much except I just kept coming second - ' He turned and gave her a funny look, '- second to last!'

'Oh,' Katrina said, smiling broadly. 'And the law degree? Dare I ask?'

'I hated it so I quit and took the first job I could find that had decent prospects, and reasonable money.' He turned to her and she gave him a look of make-believe horror, the reaction she knew he was waiting for. He smiled, 'We can't all be overachievers like you.'

Katrina laughed. 'Shame, shame!' she said, and playfully flicked her hand against his arm.

'But are you happy?' she asked.

'Yeah, pretty much,' he said. 'What about you?'

'Yeah, pretty much,' she said, echoing his tone, leaving as much as he had unsaid.

They stopped and sat on a bench overlooking the harbor, Scott stretching his arm along the railing behind her.

'I've read a lot about you in the press lately. That sounds like one helluva device you invented. You're one amazing lady, Dr Dudek.'

'Why, thank you,' she said.

'I always knew you'd do something great with your life....' His voice trailed away and Minstrel, who had been lying on the ground at his feet, sat up and burrowed his head between Scott's knees.

Katrina finished the sentence for him, 'in memory of David, you mean?'

Scott nodded wordlessly. Some yachts sailed in front of them, barely moving, their large sails straining to catch the smallest breath of wind. A ferry blasted past, the sound of its engines echoing up the hills, mocking the vagaries of nature.

Taking his arm down, Scott leant forward, resting his chin in his palms. Minstrel lifted his front paws and licked his master on the cheek. Scott turned just as she rubbed away a tear. 'And you've never gotten over him either, have you?' he said gently.

'How do you ever get over something like that?' Katrina mumbled. 'He was as much a part of me as my reflection.'

On their return home they took the short but steep route, up one hundred and thirty-eight steps, Katrina counted them all. Admiring the view from the top they waited for Minstrel to wearily pull his hind legs up the final steps. Scott moved close to Katrina telling her how much he'd enjoyed himself, before asking her out to dinner another night.

- 20 -

At the last board meeting Steen had reported an excellent reception from institutional fund managers and investment houses. In his opinion they didn't need any more publicity, with the present level of interest the stock issue would be fully subscribed when they came to launch. 'The less ma and pa investors we attract, the easier it'll be for us long-term,' he said.

Though Katrina had received hundreds of speaking invitations as a result of the press meeting, Steen advised her to decline them all, with only one exception: a closed door session in Washington with five senators on a select committee. Checking out the window, she was relieved to see the clouds barely moving as they were sending a chopper to pick her up later that afternoon and she wanted to arrive feeling calm.

Relishing the chance to influence future health economic policies, Katrina sat at her computer, reviewing some notes she'd made several months ago. First she cut and pasted a description of the Invivotest - the abnormalities they could test for now and those they'd be able to do in the near future. Then she decided to highlight the way results could be obtained early in the pregnancy allowing less time for maternal bonding. She wanted to make sure this subtle advantage wouldn't be lost on a bunch of men who mightn't understand how a mother's biological instincts can flare into action the first time she sees her baby on an ultrasound scan. If intervention was warranted, it'd be more humane done earlier rather than later.

She opened another file and copied some notes, wanting to show them how Invivotest was vastly cheaper than any other prenatal test, then she'd turn up the pressure and move onto a discussion about cost-effectiveness - they were politicians, they'd be able to handle it. She found some slides she'd never shown before and inserted them into her notes. The first slide estimated the lifetime medical costs of a normal baby versus one with cystic fibrosis then added a graph comparing the respective economic contribution of both babies. She hesitated then decided to go the whole way, importing other new slides that made a comparison between a normal child and children with Huntington's chorea and Down Syndrome. The graphs showed the average lifetime cost of caregivers, medical treatments, special education, mobility and security needs, and also the opportunity cost to society. That should get their attention!

The phone rang. It was Clint; he was now a father. She could hear the elation in his voice, the rush of new emotions adding a breathless pitch. She hung up and walked to the window wanting to stop the feelings, the twist in the stomach, the clawing heat behind her eyes. Sunlight scattered small rainbows of spray off the curves of the aluminum sculpture.

Returning to her chair, she sat down, dislodging the keyboard with her hand, knocking the glass paperweight onto the floor. Thank God it wasn't broken! She picked it up; the glass felt cold, the needle wobbled due north.

For the last time she turned her attention back to the computer and reread her speech, her eyes stumbling over the words Lifetime Cost. A whole lifetime - someone's eternity - it was cruel to make someone live that long as a burden to society.

Gemini looked over at the twins sleeping peacefully in their bassinet. They were less than thirty-six hours old yet it seemed as though they'd always existed, always been part of her alchemy.

Never before had she felt such intensity of emotion, such awe-inspiring gratitude. Tears constantly flowed down her face, her happiness prompted by a small hand unfurled in hers, a baby yawn, or a glimpse of the palest-blue irises of their eyes. It was their freshness and perfection that overwhelmed her. Every moment felt brand new.

As the effects of the painkillers started to wear off Gemini felt a lot more pain where the stitches were, and most of the first night she'd been kept awake by a succession of nurses lifting the babies to her whenever they needed breastfeeding.

Gemini finished the last of her cereal and put her bowl on the breakfast tray and pushed it away. At the sound of footsteps, she looked up to see a ward helper enter the room carrying a bunch of flowers. The woman pulled the card off the colored paper and handed it to Gemini before stuffing the flowers, complete with wrapping, into a plastic vase.

Rotating the card at different angles, Gemini read all the good wishes sent by work colleagues, and by the time she'd finished the helper had gone. With nothing else to do, Gemini gave her new flowers a closer look: a conglomeration of long-stemmed roses - orange, peach, pink, red and white - along with some silver-painted twigs and sticks for artistic effect, all wrapped in a rose-shaped scrunch of green paper. Pamela's daffodil collection looked spindly by comparison.

Gemini smiled at the recollection of Pamela's excitement, the involuntary rasp of breath inhaled and the unrehearsed exhalation of admiration - acknowledgement in full that she'd received the gift of grandchildren.

Comfortably propped up in bed, Gemini closed her eyes and savored the precious quietness with both babies still asleep. She must have dozed off, because the next thing she was aware of was a bump on the bed and the touch of lips on her cheek.

Pamela took the only seat in the room and moved it up near the head of the bed, and while Gemini reluctantly regained consciousness she explained Clint was parking the car.

Side on, Gemini saw Pamela's eyes moisten as they focused on the babies in the bassinet but oblivious to the attention, both babies continued sleeping.

Pamela opened her handbag and passed an envelope to Gemini. 'Here's something from Hudson and Greg. They send their love of course.'

'Thanks.' Gemini reached inside the envelope and pulled out a card, along with some money. *Congratulations, sis, rather you than me! I didn't know what to get you - please buy something you like for the babies. Lots of love, Hudson and Greg.*

'He'll never go wrong with that present! As it happens I know one thing I want - I saw them in a shop the other day.' Gemini told her mother about two hand-embroidered baby blankets that had caught her attention: one with ladybirds embroidered across it, the other with bumblebees. Describing the shop's location, within walking distance from her home, she gave Pamela the money to buy them.

Clint hurried in, carrying several more bunches of flowers, and when Pamela saw they needed some vases she politely left the room to give them a few moments to be on their own.

After they'd chatted for a while Clint handed Gemini a parcel he'd brought with him - a lavishly wrapped gift from Katrina. Gemini carefully untied the ribbon, gasping when she pulled back the silver-blue paper to reveal two blankets: one embroidered with bumblebees, the other with ladybirds.

At work, in the shower, in the car, at lunchtime, bedtime and other times too, Katrina rehearsed what she was going to say, but now she was sitting at a table in a Chinese restaurant not far from Scott's house she couldn't remember exactly how it all went.

Why, Katrina wondered, did she feel compelled to tell Scott the truth that he might not have been the father - when he'd probably never find out? There seemed to be no logical answer, just a feeling that needed to be obeyed. And underpinning it all was the realisation she wanted someone in her life, and he was sensitive and sincere, like no other man she'd met before, or since.

Two candles flickered in crystal flower-shaped holders between them, their flames filling the awkward moments with movement. It seemed the waiter had only just taken their order when he returned with a plate of spring rolls and sauces, and Katrina sensed Scott was as grateful as she was for the interruption.

Unfolding the linen napkin, Katrina waited for the right moment to speak, and in that short pause Scott seized the initiative. 'About the twins,' he said, 'do you know what happened to them? Did you ever try looking for them?'

'No,' she said, the single syllable sounding too stark. Adding, 'No, I haven't.'

His eyes narrowed and disapproval flickered in his eyes, she could almost see the conclusions he was drawing - that she'd blocked the twins out of her life, she was cold and heartless. She reached for her wineglass, lifting it to her lips, wishing she'd led this conversation.

'Didn't you think to call me,' he said, 'to at least tell me about the twins…before you did what you did?'

In the pause that followed she felt his condemnation: If she'd withheld that information, what else was she capable of not telling him? How could he ever trust her? What a fool she'd been to think they could have a future together. Taking a deep breath she steadied her nerves.

'Would you really have wanted to have known,' she said, in her very softest tone, 'even if you might not have been the father.'

Scott gasped. A look of disbelief followed by irritation flashed in his eyes. 'I didn't know you'd been seeing anyone else,' he said.

'I wasn't,' she said, her voice close to a whisper. 'I was raped.'

Rape was the closest word she could think of to describe what she had done to her soul. The truth, she acknowledged, was Bob had only been an accomplice and though he was older than her and should've known better, it was rape all right - they'd raped each other. Too late now to retract her words, Katrina stared into the purple centre of the flame, closing her mind to any further debate.

The candle shed soft shadows of light between them, and she waited, half-expecting him to leave. How was a man supposed to react to the news of a violation that had occurred to someone he'd cared for in the past? Should he be angry, hurt or disbelieving? Or didn't it matter so long after the event?

'So they weren't mine,' he said. She could see his numbness, his mind trying to make sense of the new reality, untangling, rearranging impressions of the past.

She shrugged, there was nowhere left to hide.

The waiter brought their meals to the table but they barely touched them. For a long while neither spoke, and when the diners behind them burst into a loud rendition of 'Why Was She Born So Beautiful' followed by loud laughter, clapping and the clinking of glasses, they got up from their table and left.

On the drive back Scott had hardly spoken and refused the offer of coffee; and when Katrina leaned over to kiss him goodnight, he simply brushed his lips against her cheek, kissing her like a brother.

In her mind she remembered how he'd looked when she told him the twins weren't his, trying to imagine what he might have felt: disappointment, longing, loss?

At the first signs of dawn Katrina put on her bikini and went upstairs to the rooftop. She tossed her towel onto a chair and in a single continuous movement dived into the pool and swam to the bottom, feeling the smooth surface slither beneath her. Touching the wall at the end with her fingertips, she turned, still kicking underwater, feeling the pressure of her pulse mounting inside her head, her lungs swelling, she battled to stay under until she couldn't any longer. Stroking powerfully towards the surface, for ten minutes or more, she idly floated on her back completing several long, slow, contemplative laps. Like leaking uranium, would her future always be tainted by the infinite half-lives of her past?

Only minutes after she'd returned to her room Scott phoned. He was sitting in his car on the road outside; he wanted to talk. She buzzed security and told them to let him in, fighting the urge to dash into the bathroom to tidy her appearance, preferring instead to retain the honesty of the moment and meet him as she was: wet hair wrapped in a towel turban, eyes still bloodshot from the pool.

Kissing him gently on the cheek, she pointed him in the direction of the sofa, noticing he wore the same clothes he'd had on the night before.

'It looks like you couldn't sleep either,' she said. 'I imagine you want to know who did it?'

He nodded stiffly. 'It was Bob,' she said, finally.

'Your father's friend?' he said. 'That sleaze?'

Shriveling inside, she forced herself to not look away.

'I'm sorry, I never knew, I never thought…'

'There was nothing you could've done,' she said.

'How could he do that to you!' Scott snapped. 'The fucking bastard. If only I'd known… ' His voice faltered, and his eyes watered then he hunched over, hiding his face in his hands.

Katrina moved over to sit beside him, hugging his shaking body from the side, feeling such indescribable shame. When she could bear it no longer she released her hold. She stood and headed towards the kitchen, parched. Gulping down a glass of water, she dawdled, her mind whirring as she tried to fathom why what had once seemed so logical, now deserved such pain. Without even knowing she was doing it, she emptied the dishwasher, mechanically stacking dishes and glasses in cupboards, before filling a glass with water and taking it through to Scott.

She entered the room, and he looked up before standing to take the glass from her and placing it on the coffee table, taking her in his arms instead. For a while he held her close and she felt his anger and regret, along with her own spiraling, sickening sense of loss. Would he never be able to love her now, was it all too late?

- 21 -

After five days of hospital food Gemini couldn't wait to get the twins home. She was looking forward to sleeping in her own bed, and knew Pamela would have prepared a special meal to welcome her back.

Flame lay in the bassinet sucking quietly on a pacifier while Gemini dressed Orion. Clint bundled two bunches of flowers together then emptied the water into the sink.

A nurse entered the room to check Gemini's wound as well as finalising the twins' charts before she discharged them.

'Don't forget we need you to sign the consent form for the babies to have their PKU,' the nurse said, showing Gemini a small sheet of blotting paper with some specially marked test sites. 'We just do a simple heel prick to get a blood sample to send off to the lab.'

Gemini signed the forms.

'The incidence of PKU is extremely low, you'll only hear back from us if we need to retest,' the nurse said, tucking the papers into Gemini's file. 'Who shall I do first?'

'Do Flame, she's the easiest to settle down,' said Gemini.

Following the nurse's instructions, Gemini held Flame tightly while the nurse pricked Flame's heel then squeezed it, smudging some blood onto the card. Flame screamed, angrily thrashing her leg about.

The nurse turned to Clint and took hold of Orion's foot and pricked it. Orion screwed his face and started bellowing his face turning purple with rage. Shaking his leg, the blood flowed freely, easily filling the entire blotting paper. Putting the card to one side, the nurse pressed a cotton wool dressing against the steady flow, only lifting the padding to check the bleeding every ten seconds or so.

'Sssshhh, ssshh, young man,' she crooned, pointlessly against Orion's ear-piercing cries. Clint smiled awkwardly and rocked Orion in his arms.

Lifting the dressing again, the nurse seemed surprised the bleeding hadn't stopped. Some blood ran down the back of her hand, across her wrist, leaking a small pool onto the waistband of her uniform. Reaching for a sterile swab, she grabbed another, and another, her face frozen in controlled calm.

Eventually she said, 'I'd like to get a doctor to have a quick look at this young fellow.' Clint passed the crying baby to her. Bundling Orion against her chest, she reapplied another swab to his heel. 'Wait here, I'll be back in a moment,' she said, striding out the room, Orion's cries echoing down the hallway.

In a whisper Gemini asked, 'What's wrong with him? He shouldn't be bleeding like that, should he?' It had all happened so quickly and was so unexpected, she still couldn't comprehend anything could be seriously wrong.

Clint shrugged. He pulled a paper towel from the basin and stooped to wipe some blood spots from the floor. Some way down the hallway they could still hear Orion's annoyed cries.

After a few minutes the cries subsided, though whether he'd stopped crying or had gone out of earshot they didn't know. Powerless to do anything, they sat and waited. Gemini watched the clock - five minutes, ten, eleven, twelve, nearly thirteen minutes - until the nurse returned with Orion asleep in her arms.

Giving them a bright smile, she tiptoed towards the bassinet mouthing 'Ssssshh, he's fine'. She carefully placed Orion next to his sleeping sister and stepped back quietly, gesturing to Gemini and Clint to follow her so they could talk without waking the babies. She told them then that the doctor had sent out some blood samples but the results wouldn't be back until the next day.

Gemini tried to read the nurse's expressionless face. 'What do you think - '

The nurse cut her off. 'Just to be on the safe side we'd like to keep

Orion in for observation, at least one more night. Doctor will be able to answer all your questions, he'll be along to see you shortly.' And with that she started to walk away.

- 22 -

Clint slammed the car into gear and put his foot down hard, pulling out of the hospital driveway with a roar. Somewhere behind him he heard a car horn blast long and loud, and though he didn't check his rear-vision mirror he knew he was the culprit. *Too bad! Too fucking bad!*

He'd waited hours to hear the results of Orion's tests, too worried before the diagnosis to eat and too upset after. Now his stomach was empty, churning through bile, burning acid. He screwed his eyes against the headlights of oncoming cars and tried to calm himself. He'd been told Orion had a blood clotting disorder, hemophilia.

The stream of headlights seemed to blur and he opened a window to let some cold air in, to try and dry his tears. A pulse throbbed across his temple and he pulled over to the side of the road to park the car, his shoulders shuddering as he let out his grief.

Plenty of people live with hemophilia he told himself, there's no point denying the diagnosis. His life may have changed but they would cope. He opened the glove box to search for his migraine tablets, his hands shaking as he pushed two white tablets through the metallic foil. Placing them in his mouth, he felt them stick to the back of his throat; momentarily thinking he was going to choke to death, he concentrated all his attention on summoning enough liquid to swallow. Mind over matter, mind over reflux, nature's way of focusing on the details of staying alive; life was something that couldn't be taken for granted anymore.

He sat a while in the timeless space of a car going nowhere. Other cars raced past, their headlights invading his privacy, a collision about to happen until they flashed past, the noise taking the light with them.

Orion, I'm so sorry. Clint took a deep breath and turned the ignition on and when the road was clear got back into the flow of traffic. He sighed, drummed his fingers on the steering wheel. Sorry for what? Sorry he'd failed this small boy? Sorry he'd done this to him - or was he just plain sorry for himself, for Gemini, and for their bad luck?

Turning into his driveway, he saw the windows were dark, just the outside light left on. Pamela must have gone to bed. He was glad about that; he didn't want to have to rephrase the doctor's diagnosis to help lessen her pain.

The kitchen felt airy and had a faint foreign smell, slightly morgue-like, as if he'd been away for years. He read the handwritten note on the bench: 'Tea in the oven. I hope all is well. Love, M. xxxx'

Without thinking he opened the oven door, then closed it and turned off the dial. Out of the corner of his eye he caught the flashing light on the telephone. Replaying the messages, he heard Gemini's voice. 'Hi, Mom, I thought you might beep-beep-beep-beep.' Pamela must have picked up the phone - so she knew. He felt another enduring pang of sadness as he thought how she must've gone to bed trying to block out the new reality that was never going to go away.

The second message was Sarah. One of the agencies had pulled out of the pitch, the other was ready to present, and she wondered if he could make it to a midday meeting tomorrow. 'Sorry,' she said, 'but Katrina wants to see what they've done in case we need to brief another crowd. I hope everything's going all right…Bye.'

After the events of the last few hours it seemed too soon to be thinking about work. He'd decide in the morning. In the meantime he needed some sleep.

Clint woke early, feeling stronger, which he knew he had to be. Gemini needed him, Flame and Orion too. Pulling on his tracksuit and running shoes he headed outside, the early morning sky was still dark but cloudless and settled and he felt a sense of peace at the sound of his footsteps crunching the sand as he broke into a gentle run.

Returning home, he fixed breakfast then checked the time. It was only 6:00 a.m., still too early to go to the hospital. Since the office was closer, and the traffic would be congested he decided to call into Inuterogene on the way. That way he could catch up on events before the midday meeting.

Drinking the last of his coffee, he heard shuffling noises coming from Pamela's room. He scribbled a note: 'Thanks for tea. Sorry I had to leave early, hope you don't mind catching a cab. Thanks again. Love, Clint.' He folded a fifty-dollar note inside the letter before rushing out the door.

It was daylight when Clint pulled into work, parking his car beside Michael's, the only other one there. The nightlights were still on in the fountain but when he looked at the double-helix sculpture, instead of pride he felt despair.

Clint entered the building and headed towards his office. Passing outside Michael's door he stopped and nearly went in, then thought better of it. What could he say, the father of twins, to the man who feared he might never have a child?

He felt guilty, then angry. By now all his colleagues would know about Orion, he'd have to face their pity or denial. Instinctively he knew he'd be expected to remove *their* fears, to reassure them he could cope. It's not natural for anyone to offer congratulations then temper it with restraint.

Though it was only five days since he'd last been in his office, his desk was covered with new mail. Clint turned on his computer and while he waited for it to flare into life, he sorted through his mail: a form from the Stock Exchange; interview appointments with new staff; some printing quotes, press clippings and conference invitations.

His computer beeped and he accessed his e-mail noticing how everything was labeled Urgent or Important yet none of it seemed to matter much. He set about replying to his messages, at least it was something positive he could do and that made him feel better.

There was a knock at the door, and before he'd had the chance to call out Michael stepped in. 'Michael,' he said, standing to offer his hand.

They shook hands, smiling, although Michael pulled his hand away a little too soon. 'I thought I'd come and say congratulations,' Michael said, his eyes seemingly fixed on something behind Clint's shoulder. 'You must be very proud.'

'Thanks. I am,' Clint replied. Unable to resist, he turned his head to check behind him. *Nothing unusual there*. He looked back and their eyes met nervously. There was a pause, no more than a quarter-second, painful nonetheless.

'What have I missed round here?'

'Just the usual,' Michael said. 'Stefano's bleating on about the counselor issue again. If he had his way all the women would get their results hand-delivered by a doctor.'

Clint sighed. 'But we've discussed this a hundred times or more, I thought it'd been decided.' Clint pointed to a chair and Michael sat down, crossing his legs.

'There's a rumor going around that the physicians are going to petition against our direct-to-the-consumer campaign.'

'But how can they protest something that isn't even up and running yet? We don't know ourselves what we're doing.'

Michael shrugged. 'I wondered that. I think it's a load of bluff, someone's scaremongering.'

'Doesn't Stefano realise that? Why doesn't he just ignore it?' Clint asked, allowing himself to sound tired because that was how he felt; tired of Stefano and his lofty ideals.

Clint watched Michael fidget in his chair, jiggling his foot. Why did he suddenly suspect Michael had an agenda of his own? 'What's your opinion, Michael?' Clint asked, 'What's this all about?'

Michael took his time replying. 'I think Stefano has a valid point, patients need professional guidance, and from someone impartial, someone who won't judge them or decide in advance what's best for them.' He paused and their eyes locked in a stare that bridged volumes of unspoken sadness. 'But that's not my only concern,' Michael said, his voice hardening, sounding more urgent now. 'I'm worried about the downstream effects of a petition like that - the wrong sort of attention we'll draw to all the work we've done.'

- 23 -

Ricky from the advertising agency had already started his presentation when Clint rushed in making his apologies.

Ricky waited for Clint to take a seat, then continued his discussion of two opposing marketing strategies. The first he labeled Accentuate the Positive, where the campaign would promote the benefits of knowing in the early stages of pregnancy that everything was normal. He showed some pictures of smiling pregnant women, some holding hands with their handsome husbands, others cradling their newborn babies, each of the headlines suggesting that none of this would have been possible were it not for Invivotest.

'Or we have a second approach,' Ricky said. 'Let's call it Eliminate the Negative.' The screen showed a slide of some crutches, a wheelchair and a sleeping baby in the background. The headline said: 'Some things in life just aren't fair.' The next visual was of the sleeping baby with a superimposed graph showing divorce statistics of parents with children with disabilities.

No one in the room moved.

Another visual lit the screen - a pregnant woman waiting at a bus stop holding her belly, a school bus in the background, its destination panel read Special Needs.

Silence lingered like a chill.

Stefano broke it. 'They're awful, surely you all think that.'

Katrina sat with her elbows resting on the table, returning his gaze she nodded slowly. Stefano looked over at Dwayne who shrugged; he didn't look happy.

'Michael?' Stefano asked.

'They're dreadful,' he said, straightening in his chair. The movement triggered a spate of shuffling, and the others joined in expressing their disapproval.

Ricky clapped his hands to get their attention. 'I take it we have approval to proceed with the first approach, is that right?'

They all agreed, and for the next half-hour Ricky discussed advertising in women's magazines, newspapers, the medical press, television and some radio. He also proposed a website and a direct mail campaign to doctors, and just before he left the meeting he asked for confirmation on the size of their advertising budget.

'That will depend on how well we do next week,' Katrina said, pausing long enough to give the public stock offering the respect it deserved. 'After what you've shown us, we'll want every cent we can get.'

On Saturday afternoon, seven days into their new lives, the babies crossed the threshold of their new home. Once they'd been settled into their nursery, Gemini, Clint and Pamela popped the cork off a cold bottle of champagne and toasted the twins' good health. Gemini had taken less than three sips from her glass when Orion woke, which in turn wakened Flame.

The treadmill of never-ending chores had just begun, with Pamela proving to be an accomplished diaper changer, bottle-maker, baby bather, cook and cleaner.

Gemini was grateful to have her there, and at times she was indispensable, like in the middle of the night when both babies woke screaming with hunger. Pamela would help latch the twins' floppy heads onto Gemini's sore, lumpy breasts, or bottle-feed the babies when Gemini was just too tired or her milk was in short supply. For the first two weeks the twins slept no more than three hours in one stretch, so the night was a continuous loop of feeding, changing, winding and rocking. After hours of walking around the living area, stroking their backs, trying to get them to sleep, sometimes Gemini had no choice but to lie them down still crying and leave them to it.

With each passing day Gemini became less intimidated when handling Orion although there were occasions her confidence in her mothering skills was shaken, such as when she lost her firm hold on Orion in the bath, his elbow banging against the side and swelling visibly before her eyes. And when she accidentally bumped his head when fixing the baby seat into the car. His body was a sea of yellow and purple bruises, small incidents any other mother would be able to disregard left lingering doubts and guilt: had she done more serious damage underneath? Her nerves were continuously stretched taut, and she knew that somehow she was going to have to learn to live with this or the stress would become too much for her.

- 24 -

The twins were almost a month old and Gemini was physically and emotionally exhausted, but she'd finally taken the first step towards confronting her future by phoning the liaison officer for the Newport Hemophilia Society: Adam Bryant.

Gemini parked the car. The quietness seemed surreal. This was the first time since the twins had been born that she'd been out without either of them. For a moment she fought an irrational panic to return home then she calmed herself, Pamela would cope.

The concrete-block apartments were a drab gray with rusty steel roofing, run-down and cheaply made. Locking her car, she noticed there were no signs of children, trees or flowers, practically no sign of life at all. She opened a steel gate and walked past the first two units with their peeling wood-varnished doors, and rapped hard on Adam Bryant's door. She heard some footsteps and the key turning in the lock before the door swung open and Adam welcomed her inside. About the same age and height as her, with close-cropped hair, he wore a plain white t-shirt and jeans, and his handshake felt firm and sincere making her warm to him straight away.

Once inside, she found the apartment was surprisingly spacious with very little furniture except for a large bookshelf, and only a spartan selection of possessions on display. Fresh air and sunlight streamed through open French doors, and outside, a rainforest mural was painted onto the concrete-wall that surrounded a small patio area filled with brightly glazed pots containing palms and a vivid display of tropical flowers.

Gemini sank into the chair she was offered. Two large woollen Nepalese rugs hung on the walls either side, and sewn amongst the red, green, blue and yellow stripes were some large reflective sequins that sparkled brilliantly, brightening the room.

To ease into a conversation, Gemini enquired about the wall hangings. 'Did you get them from Nepal yourself?'

'I wish,' Adam said, walking over to the bookshelf, straightening some books. 'The closest I've got to Nepal, or anywhere else exotic for that matter, is the Trade Aid store and the Sunday markets.'

'Sorry, I never thought, can't you travel overseas?'

'Not really. Hemophilia is a bad risk as far as health insurance goes,' he said. 'Take a look at those books over there while I make the coffee.'

Gemini browsed through the bookshelf and selected a hardback with lots of glossy photographs inside. Turning the pages, she forced herself to look at the images of bruising, and the permanent damage of deformity and arthritis done to joints.

Adam returned, placing their drinks on a small table between them. 'A lot of those are worst case scenarios,' he said, glimpsing the page that was opened on Gemini's lap. 'The most common bleeds are into joints, or soft tissue and muscle. They're painful, but if treated properly, permanent damage can usually be avoided.' He paused to sip his coffee, giving her time to absorb the information. 'I think you're doing the right thing learning what you can now. Some of the worst incidents happen to those who've hardly had any effects until one day, whammo, they have an accident and suddenly no one knows what to do. You need to take responsibility for the disease yourself, and you need to know the signs to look for because occasionally life-threatening situations do occur if the bleeding obstructs an airway, or there's a hemorrhage into a major organ.'

Life-threatening. Gemini closed the book and put it on the table; there was no room in her life now for squeamishness and cowardice if she was to provide the best care for Orion.

'Do both your twins have it?' he asked.

She shook her head. 'No. Just the boy.'

'How bad is he?'

She shrugged. 'The doctors don't know for sure. It's too early to say.'

'It's hard on children,' Adam said. 'The restrictions on sports and activities, the protective clothing, the teasing…'

Gemini felt sick to her stomach as she visualised her darling Orion being ridiculed for not being able to play sport in ways other kids took for granted.

'I've got a lot to look forward to,' she said, with a light laugh that wobbled falsely, undoing her attempt to reassure him she could handle it.

'I know I'm not painting a blue-skies picture - and you never know you might be lucky - but on the other hand, would I want to change the way I am? This is a part of who I am and what I am. In some ways the disease has made me experience a spiritual dimension I might never have known otherwise.'

He looked intently at her. 'What about you - do you have any spiritual or religious beliefs?' It felt as though he was staring right through her, piercing her soul. He didn't wait for a reply, asking instead: 'Have we met before?'

She shook her head slowly. 'I don't think so.' He didn't seem convinced, so just to be polite she added, 'Perhaps I have a double.'

He dropped his gaze. 'You're a twin, aren't you?' he asked.

'How did you know that?'

'I just had a funny feeling. And anyway, you're the mother of twins so I had a good chance of being right!'

He asked about Gemini's twin, and laughed at her description of Hudson's flamboyant sexuality and how it bothered her mother. For a while they chatted about twins, genetics was a subject that interested him.

'And what about you, did anyone else in your family have it?' Gemini asked.

Adam shook his head. 'It's a mystery. There's no family history, but that's the power of nature, isn't it? All it takes is one fluke gene or genetic mutation.'

'Are you married?' she asked. She didn't think he'd mind her asking.

'I was…but she died this time last year.'

'I'm sorry.'

As if he needed to tell her, he went on, 'There's no need to be. It was cancer. I met her up at the hospital. We were only married six months, and we both knew she didn't have long to go…'

He went to the kitchen and came back with a photograph of a bald-headed woman with big brown eyes but no eyebrows. 'This is Bridget. I don't leave her on display, I don't need to remember what she looked like. I prefer to remember her presence - the way she thought, the things she said, the feelings we had for each other.'

Gemini blinked back tears. Adam looked up and laughed gently. 'You big softie, you never even met her!'

'I know, it's just so sad.'

He took the photo back to the kitchen, lifting the picture to his lips, lightly kissing the flat glossy surface.

'Excuse me,' she mumbled, standing quickly, blindly making her way out onto the patio where she pretended to admire a plant.

When she returned she simply said, 'Sorry.' Somehow she knew he'd understand. He handed her a box of tissues and she dabbed at her eyes while he carried on talking as if nothing had happened.

'Hemophiliacs make up a small community and death is something we get used to - in our newsletter we always have two or three obituaries. I know this might sound morbid to you but I've planned my funeral, written my own remembrance speech, and even included a list of people to invite. I want it to be a celebration of life. I think death helps bring life into sharper focus.'

Then he asked Gemini about her family history and she told him what little she knew of her adoption. Or at least the story of the day she and Hudson were told they were adopted because oddly that seemed to be the day the story began, though logically it'd started well before then.

Pamela was putting the twins to bed the night after their fourth birthday when she told them. They were so tired from a witch and wizard party - complete with hedgehog pie, vomit soup and a cake decorated with marzipan frogs' legs and cats' eyes - the news barely registered. But after that, whenever Gemini tried to talk to Pamela about it she found the subject was closed. And Hudson didn't seem interested - to his way of thinking his mother was Pamela, what else was there to discuss?

'I've read more women than men search for their mothers,' she said. 'I guess it's just more important to us.'

'It's hard to generalise,' Adam said. 'My dad left when I was two years old; my Mom's missed out on a lot because of me…'

It felt like time to leave. Gemini thanked Adam for his hospitality and asked to use his bathroom. On her way down the hallway she noticed a print of the yellow tortoise, the same as the one she'd bought Clint. There's no such thing as coincidence, she thought, the picture was a sign, although of what she wasn't sure. Returning to the lounge, she invited him around one day to meet the twins. He wrote her address on a notepad then showed her to the door. 'Are you sure we haven't met before?'

'Not that I can recall,' she said, knowing it would have been impossible to meet him and not remember his intense blue eyes.

- 25 -

Pamela returned to Palm Springs when the twins were six weeks old, and for a while Gemini barely coped. There were days she didn't care that Clint came home to a scene of devastation: towels lying on the floor, an untidy kitchen bench, and a laundry basket full of washing and piles of unfolded clothing heaped nearby. Auspicious or inauspicious, she was too tired to care.

She was also getting increasingly frustrated at the days and nights Clint was spending away from home on the financial roadshow to promote the public stock offering. But when they were together she'd find it even more annoying that they couldn't have a conversation without one of the twins interrupting them with their cries. It was hard to accept that the last intelligent conversation they'd had was over six weeks ago, before the twins were born, and she worried it might have been their last moment of intimacy for some time yet to come.

Sitting on the sofa feeding Orion, Gemini listened to the sounds of Clint getting up; she could tell he was rushing, running late. When he appeared he was fully dressed, and she smelt the watery scent of his shaving cream as he leant over to kiss her good morning before hurrying out the door. Gemini didn't get up; she was numb from tiredness after the night before when she'd spent hours walking the living room floor as Orion kicked his legs in pain, his face purple from screaming. Now Orion was calm she felt his temple; he didn't appear hot, but she decided to phone the medical center just to be sure.

The door had closed behind Clint, who was heading for the airport, and suddenly Gemini regretted not giving him more attention. Today was the day Inuterogene was to publicly list on the NASDAQ, the day that marked the culmination of all his hard work and it seemed unforgivable she should have kissed him so dismissively. She wanted to phone him to give him her love, but Orion was on the point of falling asleep in her arms - that call to Clint would have to wait.

At the NASDAQ Stock Exchange a cheer went up as the letters INUT lit up on the board. The official stock ticker-code for Inuterogene flashed its presence as if it had always been there, always would be.

The session started with bids around $15.00. Swept up in the excitement of the moment, Katrina, Clint and Steen patted each other's backs and hugged like drunken hooligans after a football match, their emotions palpable - pride, excitement, joy, apprehension and exhilaration, but most of all relief. Until the launch, success had been hypothetical; but now they had proof other people believed in them. They would succeed.

In the first hour of trading the shares rose to $21.00, then settled down around $19.00 before closing at $19.50.

For Clint and Katrina the day was an epic procession of handshaking photo opportunities and hype; they were involved in a live internet broadcast, had interviews with various members of the Stock Exchange and the financial press, and got a small mention in a televised business report. The company had already received ratings recommendations from stockbrokers, three rating INUT as Buy and one rating it a Strong Buy.

At lunchtime Clint managed to break away long enough to phone Gemini, disappointed to find she wasn't there, he left a message telling her he'd be late home.

In the dim yellow light of the back seat Clint was having difficulty seeing how many dollar notes he had in his hand. He settled for giving the driver a handful and told him to keep the change, guessing by the respectful grunt he'd been more than generous, a trait of the tired drunk.

Clint hadn't known when he left home that morning that Steen had booked a private room for a champagne celebration with as many of the leading fund managers he could find to invite. The event had degenerated into a night of brandy shooters, bragging, bawdy jokes and gossip. Now, at three o'clock in the morning, Clint's befuddled mind could only focus on one thing; a rumor that Zenogen had appointed a former First Lady to be the spokesperson for their advertising campaign.

Fumbling his keys in the door, he shoved it open and stumbled inside. Zenogen, what was it about them? Why was everyone so vague on the details? They were an unlisted private company, supposedly a joint venture between two private companies that were both small players in their fields, neither having a reputation for innovation nor for the sort of revenue stream that could fund much of a research and development department. So where was their funding coming from? And the First Lady, did they *really* have that much clout?

Gemini wakened at the first sound of a car door slamming before the driver revved its engine and raced off into the night. She heard keys jingling in the lock, someone crashing down the hallway. *He's drunk; he'd better not wake the babies up.* She lay stiffly in bed, hearing the cistern in the bathroom whoosh and gurgle with great surges of sound that could only be that loud, she thought, if the door had been left wide open.

Her mind fumed with resentment; lately he'd hardly spent anytime with the babies, he was always at work. Hearing Clint return to the living room she guessed he was going to sleep out there for the night.

***

At work the next day Clint read the e-mail from Dr Silvano then picked up the phone to arrange to take him to lunch.

In the café light Clint thought Stefano looked younger somehow, more vital than usual.

'I woke up one day and decided I missed being a doctor,' Stefano said, his eyes sparkling with what they both knew to be the irony of the situation.

'Oh yeah, pull the other one, its got bells on it,' Clint said. He'd often been on the receiving end of Stefano's long raves about how he'd hated being called to help a woman in labor just when his dinner was on the table or as he was having a long relaxing bath. 'So you're going to give up your independence and go back to a life of servility?'

'That's the one!'

'Really?' They looked at each other; it was time to stop fooling around.

'Absolutely. When I left medicine to go into clinical research I hoped I'd be able to make a bigger contribution to people's lives - but now I worry I've done more harm than good.' Stefano sipped his coffee. 'I don't support your decision to offer the Invivotest without full genetic counseling, and I never will.'

'I know that,' said Clint quietly, knowing he'd miss Stefano's honesty when he was gone. 'What are you going to do?'

'I'm going back to Kelston Medical. My children are older, I'll probably appreciate the job more now.' Stefano let out a happy grunt, a sort of chuckle. 'I'm looking forward to it, it's about time I caught a newborn baby.'

When Stefano spoke again he'd stopped smiling. 'Some of my friends are amazed I'm quitting. In their eyes I have it all: a well-paid position with a high-flying company, fancy title, company car, stock options, plush office, the retirement plan. But what none of them realise is it was costing me the only thing that really matters, my soul.'

He took a large bite out of his doughnut. Cream oozed up onto his lip and he wiped it off, a tad embarrassed. 'I used to think we're not our jobs, but I now see how naïve I was. Of course your job filters your life experience - it has to. Commercial cleaners can't help seeing the dust on the ledges; dentists can't stop noticing teeth that need straightening. Do you know what I'm saying, Clint? In ways you can't stop, your job gets personal.'

Clint felt a kick in his stomach. Lately he'd noticed uncertainty creeping into business decisions that used to be clear-cut. Swallowing hard he concentrated on keeping his face expressionless; his pride wouldn't let him show a reaction.

Stefano continued, 'It was affecting my attitude towards people, my children, my marriage. I feel much better now I've made the decision to go...we're all much happier now.' Their eyes met. Stefano had never before mentioned any stress at home, yet strangely Clint knew he'd known all along - it was as if divorce, or at least the threat of it, was an unspoken executive honorarium, part of the package. He suddenly got the urge to confide his own fears and worries but instead he reached over for the sugar and stirred it into his coffee.

They sat, sipping their coffees, watching people file by with trays of food. After a while Stefano said, 'It's the marketing I object to.' Clint held Stefano's gaze, battling the instinct to look away. 'If I'd known how we were going to end up promoting the test I would never have got involved.'

Clint kept quiet, not wanting to interrupt the flow.

'On that score I blame myself, I should've seen it coming. I was just being a stupid, head-in-the-sand scientist. For some reason I always envisioned the Invivotest would be used as a clinical tool to take the uncertainty out of diagnoses and to help improve treatment outcomes.'

Stefano shook his head and sighed as if he was regretting the undelivered promise of the last few years. 'I didn't foresee the sinister underside, that we would end up marketing this like some sort of cheap genetic horoscope.'

On the word 'cheap' Clint thought he heard a bitterness that hadn't been there before.

'What effect will our results have on the lives of newborns whose potential will never be given a chance because it wasn't written in their genes? And what about all the little boys who'll have to spend hours working out on the track because their parents were told they have a superior athletics gene?'

A shiver ran down Clint's spine. He'd once shared his personal story with Stefano and now it'd been used like a spear to puncture him.

'But we don't provide that level of information,' Clint said.

'Not yet, you mean,' Stefano said, his voice cold and emotionless. 'It's only a matter of time before that happens - because that's what the market will demand.'

For a moment Clint wondered at the depth of Stefano's hurt, how long it might take him to get over the anger he must feel for his broken dreams, if he ever would. Clint watched a waitress clear a table and just as she walked away he heard Stefano say, 'You see, Clint, I believe in a spiritual component to life. I want my grandchildren to realise their dreams, not their genetic destiny.'

Steen worked solidly in the background, schmoozing with institutional buyers and the financial press. Stocks rallied with each positive media release and broker recommendation and less than two weeks after its launch the stock was trading as high as $28.00. The compliments were rolling in and a buzz of excitement filled the air, even outsiders would have heard it in Sarah's voice as she answered the phones. Like a communicable disease, it was infectious.

The sudden cash injection instantly increased activity. Container loads of DNA chips were trucked into the warehouse to be unpacked, and almost overnight the rear carpark was filled with the vehicles owned by the factory staff who were employed to manually assemble and pack the Invivotest.

Jackson was kept busy reviewing submissions from trucking and distribution firms, Dwayne employed even more consultants to help him with his data encryption program, and Michael was hardly ever seen - he was in a scientist's state of nirvana now he'd got his extra funding for research.

Clint oversaw the installation of the call center and finalised advertisements, and interviewed and trained prospective staff.

The doctors' launch meeting was now less than four weeks away and Drew, the sales director, and Clint put ticks beside items in the project scheduler once they'd decided who was responsible for making sure the jobs were completed. Afterwards they discussed the roadshow of mini-conventions they were going to hold in all the main centers.

Clint handed Drew a brightly colored box he planned to send to doctors whether they'd attended a meeting or not. He wanted to be sure every single doctor in the country had received information about Invivotest, like a military operation, he was leaving nothing to chance.

Drew opened the package and studied the contents, then smiled at Clint. 'I think the doctors will be most impressed. I certainly am.'

Clint laughed. That was exactly what he liked about Drew, he was always so confident.

- 26 -

The intercom buzzer rang and Gemini went over and pushed the button.

'Hello?'

'Western Deliveries.' A small uniformed boy held his identity tag to the camera.

'Come on up,' Gemini said, pressing the button to release the security grill, letting him in.

She waited by the door as he put the arrangement of white lilies on the floor so he could pull his delivery book out of his back pocket. After signing the docket she accepted the lilies, wondering who'd sent them. It was too late for a birth acknowledgement, and there were no special occasions she could think of that warranted flowers.

'Careful,' he said. 'I think the vase is made of glass.'

The flowers were wrapped in iridescent purple paper with a string bow. She carried them inside and placed them on the kitchen bench. Inside the envelope she found a simple white card with a rainbow running across the front. It didn't contain a message on the inside, and turning it over she saw it was blank on the back also. Curious, she searched amongst the wrapping for some hint of the sender's identity but found nothing.

Deciding the florist must have forgotten to write the message, she searched for a phone number, and when she couldn't find one she looked under 'W' in the telephone book. Finding no such company, she dialed Clint.

'Did you send me flowers?'

'Not today. Why do you ask?'

Gemini told him about the delivery.

'Are you sure there's nothing on the vase? What about on the bottom?'

Taking the cordless phone over, she pulled every last piece of purple wrapping from the vase, picked it up and looked underneath.

'Nothing I can see. Hang on, it looks like there's something inside, by the stems…' She lifted the vase closer to her face. She'd often been intrigued by the clever ideas florists had; she'd seen them decorate vases with brussel sprouts, tomatoes or baby carrots to add texture and color to their designs. Something moved amid the stalks; it might have been a fish. She squinted to get a better look - there definitely was something silvery-pink and willowy entwined in the stems.

Clint heard the phone drop to the floor and some footsteps and spluttering noises as Gemini ran retching to the bathroom. His knees went weak and shaky and his palms broke out in a cold clammy sweat.

'Gem…Gem…Are you okay?'

There was no reply. Dropping the phone back on the stand, he grabbed his jacket and was bolting out of the office when the phone rang. Hearing Gemini's voice, he breathed out a long sigh of relief.

'Gem? What is it? Are you all right?' he asked, waiting for her to control her sobs, feeling sure they were gasps of shock and revulsion, that she was in no physical danger.

'What is it, Gem? Tell me,' he pleaded.

'Th-th-there was…in the b-b-b bottom of the vase…a fetus…Quite a few. Puppies or kittens…I can't tell which…' Clint heard her cough and splutter, and then the noises were muffled; she must've put her hand over the mouthpiece, though he could still hear water running in the sink.

The hairs on the back of his neck stood up and he went all shivery. Straining his ears to identify the noises on the end of the phone, he heard her fumble with the handset and he called her name. 'Gem -

are you there?' He said it several times, at intervals, until she replied, and then he told her to stay calm. 'I'm on my way home. I'll be there as soon as I can.'

'Don't be long, Clint. Please. I'm so scared,' she said.

Clint was surprised to see a strange car in the driveway. Clint parked his car and rushed up the stairs, opening the door to see Gemini in Adam's embrace. She looked at Clint, her eyes red, face tear-stained. Clint paused at the door, subconsciously expecting her to rush to him, and when she didn't he walked over to the sink.

'Coffee anyone?' he asked, an edge of brittleness undermining his hospitality.

Adam pulled himself away from Gemini. 'Not for me, thanks,' he said. 'I was just about to leave.'

'Thanks, thanks for coming,' Gemini said, showing him to the door.

When she returned Clint was making coffee, ignoring the purple wrapping and the vase of flowers. 'I needn't have bothered to rush home, it seems,' he said icily.

'Not with that show of sympathy,' she cried, running to the bedroom, throwing herself on the bed.

Clint followed. 'I'm sorry,' he said, 'that was a little harsh. I know it's not an excuse, but I'm shocked too.' He sat beside her and stroked her shoulders and back. 'I'm sorry, Gem, truly sorry. Please will you forgive me?'

She squirmed away from his touch. 'It's not Adam you should be mad at. You should be thanking him. He's been a great friend and support to me when you couldn't be. Let's face it Clint, you're never here, and when you are your mind is still at work.'

The phone rang and neither moved to answer it. After six rings the answer machine clicked on and they heard the muffled tones of someone leaving a message, and then the shrill elongated beep and click as the machine switched itself off.

Gemini spoke first, in a voice close to a whisper she asked, 'What else might those people do? What if they want to hurt our babies?'

He knew it was inevitable she would ask. 'I doubt it,' he said. 'Whoever did this must be pro-life, so it's not going to fit their philosophy to harm us, is it?' A reasonable rationalisation, and for all he knew it could be true.

She shrugged dispassionately, and in that gesture he saw that she held no hope in his ability to fix things and he felt an overwhelming rush of guilt, that this had happened to her because of him.

'I think it's time we had a good talk, don't you?' Gemini said without emotion. Then she told him she was tired of him not being there, tired of his long hours, the little contact he had with the children, and his preoccupation with other things even when he was home. 'Do you want us to drift apart?' she asked. 'Because if you do you're going the right way about it.'

'Of course not,' he replied. 'I love you, you know that.' He got on his knees and held her hands, looking earnestly into her eyes. 'Gem, I never meant things to get like this. I know I've neglected you but it won't be for much longer. Once the product launch is over the workload will ease off, I promise.'

Gemini opened her mouth as if she was going to say something, then released her hands, shaking her head, she sighed as if there was no point talking to him, he wouldn't understand. His heart skipped a beat, and then with a thump pounded into motion again, as he realised she no longer believed him. For a moment she looked like she was going to leave the room but then thought better of it, maybe she knew she'd never have his attention more than she did right now.

But when she did look at him again his throat tightened, her eyes were dull and lifeless. He'd always assumed he had all the time in the world, she would wait for him, but now he knew he was wrong, love and immediacy are intertwined.

She didn't flinch as she told him she understood the pressure he was under, but that it was more than that. 'It's like the job has changed you.'

Her words hung in the air, echoing like coins dropped into an empty well. 'I never see you kiss the twins, spontaneously wipe their dribble, stroke their cheeks. And when you do hold them, it's stiffly - because it's your duty, not a joy. I know it all sounds so stupid when I say it like this but it's as though you've become disconnected from your feelings, as though you've sold your soul.'

His insides lurched, her words taking the same shape as Stefano's. His mind spun around and he felt as if he was inside his own dream of a dream, and when he caught sight of himself in the mirror he was surprised to see he looked so normal, nothing like how he felt. He saw his tie was crooked and put his hand up to straighten it and as he did so he had the unwanted revelation that he'd failed her. He'd always thought failure, when it came, would've been more obvious; there'd been no big bang or ooh's from a crowd, instead it had crept up behind him, catching him unawares.

He let out a noise that sounded like a hiccup, an involuntary gasp of anguish and when Gemini turned to look at him he guessed his distress must have been transparent because the pupils in her eyes softened and blurred. She offered him her hand; he took it and let her pull him beside her onto the bed. Down the hallway the twins started to make some tiny whimpering noises, a reminder that this time they had alone together had limits imposed.

'You've got it all wrong - '

'No, you listen to me. *You've* got it all wrong. We should be your top priority, and if we're not we'll find someone else who'll put us on the top of their list.' She stood up in response to the twins' cries and left the room.

Clint leant forward to get up off the bed, and then on an impulse threw himself backwards with such force he bounced once before sinking into the mattress, stunned. Never before had an argument ended in a threat.

He stared at the ceiling, listening. What was she doing now? He could hear both twins were still crying so he reluctantly went to the nursery to help. Gemini held Orion and was bouncing him up and down, whispering in his ear to calm him while Flame lay in bed, sobbing, discharge from her nose dripping onto her top lip. Clint picked Flame up and almost instantly her pitiful cries dissolved into squeals of delight.

'Should I give her a bath?' he asked.

'I thought you'd have to get back to work,' Gemini said woodenly, making him wonder if she was reminding him of his obligations or challenging him to desert her, to disappoint her yet again.

'They won't miss me so long as I'm back by three,' he said, trying to sound as off-hand as possible.

'Well, okay then, thanks.' She handed him some baby clothes and a towel.

'I do love you, you know,' he said softly.

'I know,' she said. 'It's just… I want you to act like you love me. I want to be the number one passion in your life, not second best.'

'Will you forgive me?'

'For the last time,' she said without a smile.

Clint bathed and dressed Flame before bathing Orion who chuckled delightedly as his father splashed water on his pink body. It'd been several weeks since Clint had bathed either child, and he had to admit he was surprised how much stronger and bigger they both were.

Gemini passed him some clothes for Orion, and while Clint dressed his son he told her he'd have to get back to the office. 'Are you going to be all right?' he asked.

'That's up to you, isn't it?' Gemini said, giving him a doubtful smile.

'I mean about those…' He tipped his head towards the flowers.

'Oh, yeah,' she said. 'They've made their point and I'm sure the people behind them are harmless as you say. I'll call you if I need to.'

He gave her a long loving kiss and promised to be home as early as he could. Before he left he went over to the table and picked up the vase of flowers, the card and its wrappings. 'I'll take these with me,' he said. 'In case we need them as evidence later.'

***

Clint arrived at work only minutes after a courier van had delivered a large chocolate cake. He walked into reception just as Sarah made the discovery that the cake's decoration wasn't chocolate sprinkles. According to the card they were ashes from the garden of remembrance for unborn children.

She screamed, threw the card on the floor and put her hand up to cover her mouth. Clint consoled her and sent her home before he took the cake into the boardroom, more evidence for the police to inspect.

Later he learnt that Michael's wife had also received a parcel, a butcher's apron smeared with blood but no card or note. Katrina had instructed security to phone and visit the homes of Dwayne, Jackson and Drew as well as her own in case there were any more surprises in store.

When the team convened for their meeting Katrina opened the drink's cabinet and offered them each a nip of brandy. Clint sat beside Dwayne. The seat opposite remained empty; it had unofficially become Stefano's place and was now a blunt reminder of his absence. When they were all settled Katrina reassured them the police thought the gifts were the work of activists who weren't considered dangerous. As a precaution, however, she'd made arrangements to place all their homes under twenty-four-hour surveillance.

'What we don't know yet is what damage they plan to do politically,' she said. 'These activists are obviously well informed, most of us have unlisted phone numbers, yet somehow they got our private addresses. Does anyone know how they might have got them?'

'You mean someone internally might be in on this?' asked Michael.

Katrina shrugged. 'I don't know. Does anyone else have a reasonable explanation?' She surveyed the room, her eyes stopping for a moment on the empty chair. Out of loyalty for Dr Silvano there was a defensive pause although no one said anything. She drew a deep breath and continued, 'The thing that surprises me most is that the press hasn't been swarming around already. Whoever planned this campaign has had more than enough time to get them in on the act, so why haven't they?'

Clint stopped at a shop to buy flowers on the way home, he chose a bunch of yellow roses - yellow for a new beginning - before swapping them for a box of chocolates when he thought how insensitive flowers would've been after the day's events. Back in his car again he channel-surfed the main radio stations but there didn't seem to be any broadcasts that related to the activists' campaign. He considered calling Stefano then thought better of it; once his ex-colleague found out the police had him down as a suspect he might take it the wrong way. Come to think of it, Clint thought, he was probably a suspect too; they all would be. He wondered if the surveillance Katrina had arranged was for their protection - or the company's, to reduce the risk of adverse publicity. Then he wondered if he'd always been that cynical.

The minute Clint opened the door he felt a transformation in the air. A delicious smell of pie wafted towards him and some candles burned softly in their holders on a window ledge, casting a flickering romantic ambience into the room. Gemini sashayed up to him and gave him a long loving embrace. She wore a pale pink, silk dress he hadn't seen before and the room was tidy, some piano music playing in the background. For a long time he held her, reveling in her softness, the lingering overtones of her perfume, the subtle smells of a woman, not a mother. 'I'm all yours,' she said in a voice that wasn't tense and loud because it had to compete with the noise of babies, 'or at least until eight o'clock when Adam brings them back.'

'I'm a lucky man,' Clint said.

'There's no such thing as luck,' Gemini said flirtatiously, leading him to the bedroom.

'There is for me,' Clint said, then he kissed her with an intensity of passion he'd forgotten ever existed.

Later that evening, after the twins had been returned and had gone to sleep, Clint lay in bed with Gemini in his arms. Not since way back in the pregnancy, before Gemini's body had become too cumbersome for him to hold, had they shared such intimacy and physical contact. For too long the focus had been on the pregnancy, birth and the twins.

Unable to fall asleep, Clint lay in the dark stroking Gemini's hair, letting his mind roam back to work. Were the flowers from a bunch of religious zealots, or the workings of a larger, more organised group? What plans might they have made for later on?

He thought about the stock market if word got out. Would investors get the jitters or would they think all publicity was good publicity?

- 27 -

Dwayne tore a page out of his diary and screwed it into a ball and threw it at the bin. It missed. He left it lying untidily on the floor.

Half an hour ago, Katrina had stormed into his office, interrupting his train of thought, insisting he link the Inuterogene website to the database so customers could access their results electronically. Then she'd left him to fix the problem.

'We can't make them wait to get their results in the post,' she'd said. 'It's way too slow - and besides, these days customers *expect* electronic access.'

'But I thought we'd agreed to start with offering only general information on the website, moving onto customer database access as phase two.' He'd paused, and because she still looked unconvinced he added, 'It would be completed by the end of the fourth quarter.'

'We…can't…wait…that…long,' she said icily. 'If we don't offer electronic access from the outset we'll be handing that competitive advantage to Zenogen on a plate.' She paced around his office, dark sparks flashing in her eyes, and he knew to tread carefully or he'd wind up doing whatever was necessary to pacify her.

Then the reality of what she'd just said penetrated. 'What do you mean? Do you expect us to bring the date forward, just like that?' he said, snapping his fingers to make the point.

She didn't respond, so he stared her down. 'We can't get it done any quicker.'

'I want it done,' she'd said. Ruthlessness had always been her trump card.

'It'll cost.'

'I don't care.'

'If we move too quickly we'll make mistakes.'

'You won't.'

'I have to be sure we can guarantee absolute data security.'

'Of course,' she said.

'These things take time, a lot of clever people are out there looking for a new challenge, a new site to hack into.' She didn't budge, making him worry anew that she underestimated the financial value of this information, appreciating only its clinical value.

'Other companies manage to do it,' she said. 'The banks, universities - hackers don't seem to find their way into them.'

'That's not entirely true,' he said. 'No one, *anywhere,* can guarantee they're one-hundred-percent secure. Not even the Pentagon.'

'As good as the Pentagon will be fine by me,' she said.

He shrugged, all resolve gone. 'Let me get some quotes. I'll get back to you.'

Katrina had then swooped out of his office, off to ruin someone else's day. The problem with computer non-experts like Katrina was that they didn't understand the amount of work involved in making the database hacker-proof, or how much could go wrong. Hacking was a three-trillion-dollar industry worldwide, and fifty-thousand American companies were affected annually. What gave them the right to think they should be the only company immune to attack?

For the right price, how many people would resist selling the story of a rogue gene running in the Kennedy family? What retirement home would accept a person with the Alzheimer's gene when they could take someone without it?

He was the gatekeeper of these secrets and took his responsibility seriously. Damn Katrina - doesn't she realise secrets are the last preserve of human choice? *Secrets keep capitalism alive.*

Why did she always have to be in such a hurry? Zenogen, of course!

He mimicked her voice in his mind: 'If we don't do it Zenogen will.' But what if some smart aleck hacked in and tampered with the information? The damage would be irreparable: it would be too late to fix things once the customer had had the termination, too late also once the baby was born.

Sometimes the responsibility seemed too much; he'd quit this job if he didn't need the money. Sighing, he searched his diary for the names of people to contact to get some quotes.

Katrina finished talking on the phone and hung up. The police had made it clear they had better things to do with their time than investigate a bunch of flowers, a butcher's apron and a chocolate cake that caused no physical harm. It was most likely the work of amateurs the officer had said raising his voice to be heard above the sounds of chaos in the background, 'We'll keep the file open, but I'm sure you've got nothing to fear,' he'd said, trying to get her off the line.

The trouble was, she did worry, the anonymity of the perpetrators preyed insidiously on her mind. She wondered about Stefano. Was it possible his disappointment had soured; that he hated what they were doing that much?

Katrina frowned. Earlier that morning Jackson had alerted her to a fault in a new consignment of DNA chips and she wondered if this new problem was in some way connected? Jackson was running some tests, hoping the flaw was limited to an isolated batch. She decided if the problem was more widespread, she had no option other than to delay the launch. They couldn't release a new product then issue a recall only a few days later, the media frenzy *that* would provoke was more than she could bear to contemplate.

She leant back in her chair needing a break from the stress of the build-up to the launch, she was looking forward to meeting Scott tonight; the last few weeks they'd only spoken on the phone.

-28-

Scott showed Katrina through to the hotel's VIP lounge. Before closing the door he hung a 'Do not disturb' sign on the knob. 'Being the manager has got to have some privileges,' he said.

Katrina sat on one of the burgundy velour sofas, in front of a window that looked across the city. Scott went behind the bar and fixed them both a drink, listening to the frustrations of Katrina's day.

'At least you've tested the quality of your quality control system,' he said, carrying the drinks over, then sitting beside her, his thigh touching hers. 'That's got to be worth celebrating.'

Raising his drink, they touched glasses. 'Here's to a successful launch, good luck tomorrow.'

'Thank you,' she said.

'Are you ready?' he asked.

'Pretty much,' she said. 'I'm not expecting the doctors will react quite as badly as the journalists did!'

He grinned.

'So you don't think the doctors will worry about those same things?'

'I doubt it,' she said. 'They'll see Invivotest as the valuable diagnostic tool it really is.'

Scott stretched his legs out, easing back into the sofa. 'And they *won't* accuse you of creating a genetic underclass?' he asked, his tone overly casual.

Suddenly on guard, Katrina slowed her response, her instincts warning her that if she wanted his love, this was another milestone she would have to pass.

'Why should we be held responsible for what happens in nature already?' she said, watching him for a reaction. 'If anything it's the reverse - we're giving the genetic underclass a choice, the chance to stop repeating the cycle.' Though he avoided her eyes, she knew he was listening, auditing every word.

Scott drained his drink and while Katrina felt his warm body beside hers, she felt a long lonely distance between them. 'The medical marketing machine has conned people into believing there'll be genetic solutions to fix everything - but the sad reality is a lot of people can't afford to see a doctor, never mind paying for expensive genetic engineering solutions for preborn babies,' she said, frustrated he still seemed to have the wrong impression of her.

Scott opened his mouth to speak but she didn't let him - if he wants to know her opinion, he should shut up and listen.

'Society only wants to believe in science where it suits, and when anything goes wrong everyone looks for someone like Inuterogene to blame. Unconditional love is a myth - you ask the parents of an autistic child what they think of unconditional love and I bet you they'd laugh in your face, or hit you. I truly believe it's better to cull out the hard-to-care-for babies than bring them into this world if they're not going to get their full entitlement of love and affection. To live a life feeling unappreciated and of no value is a uniquely human form of torture.'

She looked into Scott's eyes, aching for some sign that he cared, then lowered her tone and said, 'Don't you think that's what David would say, if he were here now?'

Scott met her gaze, and she waited with breathless impatience for his reply. Eventually he smiled. 'I guess you're right,' he said, and she saw then a softness in his eye, a melting.

Later that evening they went to the movies, then for a drive after. They had stopped at some traffic lights when Katrina commented on the window display in a fashion store on the corner.

'What beautiful dresses,' she said, pointing to them, 'look at that purple one - oh and that red one, with sequins, aren't they so divine?'

'I don't believe it!' Scott said, shaking his head.

'What do you mean?' Katrina asked.

'Maisonique - that was Patti's favorite store. I've been dragged in there more times than I care to remember.'

Katrina stared out the window; it was rare for him to mention Patti's name. 'What was she like?' she asked, reaching over, rubbing his neck, wondering how deeply Patti must have hurt him, begrudging her the space she'd occupied in his heart.

He snorted. 'The way I feel about her now makes that kinda hard to answer,' he said, accelerating when the lights turned green. 'We met at swimming, I liked her laugh. She was clever, good-looking, head strong - in some ways she was a lot like you.'

And perhaps that was the problem, Katrina thought despairingly, when they arrived back at her apartment and Scott left the engine running, leaning over to give her only the merest hint of a kiss, more like he was her brother.

The Eisenhower Ballroom was packed to capacity when Katrina took the podium to welcome their guests to the inaugural Invivotest medical meeting. Outlining the format for the evening, she warned there wouldn't be time to discuss ethical issues.

'I'm sure you all have a personal opinion on prenatal testing, and this will be different for each and every one of you. Tonight's event is educational, to give you the chance to ask any technical questions you may have about Invivotest's use.' She passed the microphone to Clint who gave a ten minute multi-media 'facts and figures' presentation on Invivotest before introducing their guest speaker, Dr Marc Shuler, a qualified physician and advocate who'd participated in some of the earliest clinical trials organised by Dr Silvano.

Katrina returned to her seat, looking forward to hearing Dr Shuler's speech. An immensely clever man, he had a quick wit and was also a dwarf who knew first-hand the prejudice society held against those who looked different. It had been Clint's idea to invite him to speak - a master stroke, she thought, as clearly Dr Shuler would be far more effective promoting their product than they could ever be. Watching him pace the stage, impeccably dressed, she admired the cut of his clothes, appreciating the extra effort it must take for him to follow fashion like any other regular-sized man.

The room broke out in loud laughter at his jokes about being, as he called it, a child of smaller dimensions, and later a more serious mood descended on their guests when he talked about his own decision not to father any children. Katrina suddenly felt an overwhelming surge of pride; from tomorrow, Invivotest would be available from medical stockists and pharmacies - women would now have a choice about the quality of life they could bring into the world. Women could project their own meaning on life; biology need not be destiny. *David would be so proud*.

Dr Shuler finished and Katrina thanked him and took the microphone to answer questions. The first few were about availability, clinical trial data, and the promptness, reliability and format of the test results.

A woman at the back of the room was concerned the home use of Invivotest might delay some patients from seeing their doctor. She'd seen this happen with teenagers and the home pregnancy test and the outcome of the delay had been a more serious problem: an undiagnosed sexually transmitted disease.

Katrina thanked the woman for her comments, agreeing she had valid concerns, then took a question from a red-haired man who sat in full view of everyone at the front of the room. At first she was so distracted by the timbre in his voice and the thought that he should be on the radio, that she nearly missed the gist of what he was saying. 'In any profession, once knowledge exists it has to be used. Ignorance is no excuse. I object to the introduction of this test because it'll become required use. I want everyone in this room to consider the implications, it's the start of eugenics - '

Katrina interrupted. 'Yes, thank you. I'm afraid we must stop there,' she said, noting with surprise that though he was being so scathing, she felt calm, dispassionate, fatalistic even. 'This is not the designated time for ethical issues - '

The doctor stood, waving his hands demonstrably in the air, his jacket opening revealing a mismatched patterned shirt and a multi-colored tie. 'Someone's got to stand up and be counted,' he yelled, 'we're all being brainwashed here.'

Still mesmerised by the tie, Katrina stared blankly, an unwanted image of Maggie's turquoise and orange tie-dyed dress came to mind along with her own seventeen-year old voice saying, 'I've already forgotten I had them.' Yet those babies had lived within her body for nearly nine months; they shared her DNA.

Clint joined her on the stage. 'Quiet, please,' he commanded, taking control.

The doctor continued, 'Ethically, we're on the slippery slope. 'Who's going to assist the Down Syndrome mother abort a normal child? Logically, how can you refuse - '

Clint signaled to two security officers standing at the back of the room.

Turning to look behind him, the doctor caught sight of the officers then started shouting earnestly: 'If doctors won't fight to preserve the sanctity of life then who will? Patients must not be allowed to…' The audience started talking amongst themselves and the troublemaker's voice faded into the murmuring as he was escorted from the room.

'Thank you,' Clint said loudly over the commotion. 'Thank you everyone, if I could just have your attention please,' he said again and again, but the chatter escalated and his voice could hardly be heard. Katrina lowered her microphone, and stood to one side, feeling strangely inconsequential.

Eventually the noise abated and Katrina began her final speech. 'Ever since man invented the wheel there's been opposition to progress,' she said. Someone in the audience laughed, then someone else started clapping and others joined in.

'Tonight we have shown you how Invivotest provides you with knowledge that goes well beyond that of other prenatal tests, yet the principle remains the same - to save our patients pain and suffering.' She paused dramatically knowing the moment was hers. 'It therefore saddens me that I have to defend technology because technology does not define morality. People do. We can not ignore the fact that society is changing, and as it changes the practice of medicine must too. I hope you'll join us in rising to meet that challenge, and let this new technology empower your medical practice, and the lives of your patients.'

A large round of applause filled the room. Acknowledging the commendation, Katrina bowed her head and left the stage as the caterers moved in, serving the food.

- 29 -

Gemini turned the volume up and watched the picture on the television take a wide-angle scan of the Inuterogene sculpture. The gardens were filled with protestors carrying placards, and a line of people had linked their arms to barricade the driveway.

She read some of the signs: 'Life is Cheap', 'Unborn Generations be Damned', 'Say NO to Eugenics', 'Satan's Work', 'Are You Good Enough?'

The television switched to a close-up of the reporter who pressed her microphone under the nose of a smartly dressed, gray-haired lady, apparently one of ringleaders. 'Testing is a form of fetal abuse and discrimination,' the old lady said, eloquently. 'We've already seen social endorsement of abortion for babies with Down Syndrome, now we're widening the field. That's why we're here today. To make a stand. Babies shouldn't have to compete on potential ability for the right to be born.' The camera switched to a man pushing an old-fashioned pram containing a collection of dolls' heads, limbs and dismembered torsos. He handed the reporter a leaflet which she held up to the camera, the headline read: *What's Normal?*

The reporter appeared back on screen. 'Perhaps the question should be who defines what is abnormal, and do we have the individual right to decide? These protestors say prenatal testing is a social statement; it is dehumanising. A spokesman for Inuterogene said the tests are a relevant medical device that will save many couples a lifetime of heartache, but he refused to comment on the protests.'

An advertisement came on and Gemini turned the television off.

She'd told Clint this would happen - but would he believe her? Of course not! Sadly, being proven right was no consolation for the aggravation his work had caused, nothing ever could be.

Clint looked at the small pile of mail on his desk. They were now into their third week after the product launch and despite all their marketing efforts they'd drawn a dismal response. Yesterday he'd even asked Sarah to double-check their mail wasn't going missing, but to no avail.

Switching on his computer, he thought about the protestors camped outside on the driveway. While there were fewer of them now, the fact they'd kept their vigil this long surprised him. There was one woman he always noticed; Hogsnort, he'd nicknamed her, she reminded him of a witch. This morning she'd squirted his windscreen with tomato sauce, squealing something about blood on his hands, it'd been a sight he'd sooner forget.

Clint checked the latest sales figures; still no improvement. The sales team were complaining, many of them feeling let down after all the suspense and hoopla of the launch. And now all this. *Thank God we've got the public campaign yet to come!* Then he remembered Hogsnort and all her allies and wondered how much protest activity they'd stir up then.

The phone rang, Drew calling from Boston to say he'd arranged a convention that night but the chairperson had just phoned in sick. He wanted Clint to stand in, catch the afternoon flight, and when Clint hesitated Drew quickly added, 'It'll be good for you to see what's happening in the field.'

Clint reluctantly agreed and called Sarah to arrange his flights. Then, with care, he phoned Gemini to let her know.

Earlier when he had called, Clint thought Gemini had seemed understanding, but now as she threw his overnight bag onto the bed he realised it had been a false state of calm.

'You promised me you'd spend more time with us,' she said, pulling some shirts out the closet then chucking them at him. 'It's never going to end, is it?'

'I have to go,' he said, 'they need me.' As soon as he'd said it, he wished he hadn't. Gemini gave him a filthy look then stormed out of the room.

Clint packed his bag and placed it by the door. He could hear a toy being squeaked in the nursery, and the sounds of a baby making his first attempts to imitate sound. Pushing the door ajar, he peeped around. 'I'm off now,' he said. Gemini got up from her place on the floor, handing Orion the brightly colored squeaky toy and giving Flame a rattle. Quickly stepping outside, she and Clint tiptoed down the hallway.

'I'm sorry about this, Gem. I promise I'll make it up to you later. I just need a bit more time and then - '

'More time!' she screeched.

He blanched at the unexpected volume. Down the hallway a small voice cried, joined by another.

'There'll never be more time than what we have now,' she said. 'You can't put real life on hold indefinitely, we won't wait for you forever…'

Her voice started to wobble, and he felt ashamed.

'You promised you'd spend more time with us once you'd launched Invivotest. You've done that and you're still not here.' Her eyes narrowed and he felt daggers pierce his soul. 'Isn't it about time you stopped believing your own lies? No one can save time. You can't go back and reclaim the first few weeks of our babies' lives, time you've spent traveling around the country…' she let her voice trail off as the twins' screams hit a higher pitch.

'Since they've been born you've barely seen them.' She spat the words out. 'Where is all that time you've saved? There must be vast bunkers of it - graveyards - stored around the countryside. I'm warning you, Clint, if you're not careful you'll have left it too late.' She turned towards the wails that echoed down the hallway. 'You'd better get going or you'll miss your plane.' Her voice was flat and final.

- 30 -

Gemini woke to the distressed cries coming from down the hallway. She glanced at the bedside clock and groaned, it wasn't even three hours since the twins had been put to bed. Cocking her head to listen, she realised Orion was crying, his cry was always the most strident.

She hurried to get him before he could wake Flame. Taking him to the kitchen to warm his bottle she felt him wrestle against her as if he had stomach pains. When the milk was heated she sat on the sofa to give him his bottle. He sucked a little, pulled his head back, cried, and took another suck before pulling away again, lifting his legs up to his groin and kicking violently. Gemini put the bottle down, stood up and placed him over her shoulder, glad when it seemed to settle him for a bit.

Wondering if he needed changing she went into the nursery and took the cane tray that held the diapers, baby powder, oils and creams back to the lounge. She spread a folded towel on top of the coffee table, as she'd done so many times before, and laid Orion down and knelt beside him. The tiles felt cold now they'd lost the heat of the day.

Orion writhed awkwardly and she hurried to undo his diaper. With one hand she held the loose flap against his tummy, and with the other she reached behind for the tray. In that same instant Orion kicked both heels against the table top, straightened his legs and lurched backwards, falling head first off the table. Gemini heard a succession of bumps as parts of his body slithered and banged against the table leg on the way down. Then a heavy thud as his body hit the floor and stopped moving, and in her ragged scramble, on hands and knees, Gemini felt a whole lifetime drop away.

Picking him up from the floor, she leaned back on her heels, feeling his limpness. His head flopped back over her lower arm, his neck limp and his eyes rolled to one side, staring without meaning. Lying him back on the ground she turned his wrist to feel for a pulse, then she leant forward and pressed her ear against his chest to listen for a heartbeat, a breath. She tapped his chest gently with her fingers, closed her lips over his nose and mouth and blew air into his flaccid body. But there was nothing; and with that recognition came the panic.

Leaping up, she took a step to the right, then faltered, her mind fumbling the decision which way to negotiate the coffee table. Stumbling to the phone, she grabbed it, her fingers numb as she punched the numbers, her hands shaking uncontrollably as she held the speaker to her mouth, and then she gagged just as the operator answered. She cupped a hand over her mouth, lifting it just long enough to give the details she was asked for, and vomited as soon as she'd hung up.

Still retching, she went back to the table and with the towel tried to roughly wipe the stains from her front before gently lifting Orion to hold him closely in her arms. Before too long she heard sirens screaming on the road below and the room was lit in a strobe effect by the flashing red lights that rotated around the walls and ceiling. She picked herself off the floor and pushed the security button and waited by the door to let the medics in.

One of the medics handed his medical kit to Gemini in exchange for Orion and then, as if it were all part of the same moment, he gave Gemini a look that confirmed his instant comprehension: they were there too late.

Stepping towards the kitchen table, he placed Orion on top and with two fingers of two hands he pumped the baby's chest, to no avail. Gemini worked her mouth to answer his questions, trying to tell him the order of things that had happened; and all the time she watched, mesmerised by a small trail of dribble that rolled down the side of Orion's mouth and along his chin. She didn't hear the other medic as he spoke on the phone and when he came up behind her and tapped her on the shoulder she jumped with fright. Taking the phone she uttered a few simple words before collapsing into the medic's arms.

Clint hated being in Boston. He was worried by Gemini's last words. How many more chances would she give him? He was gambling with her affection, acting like his father's son. Especially in the quiet moments of the journey his thoughts had become obsessive, and he was glad that as soon as he arrived Drew had got him involved in preparations for that evening's meeting.

He was brushing his teeth when the phone rang, thinking about his father again: what if there was a gambling gene? A competitiveness gene? An addiction gene? There were traits in himself he didn't much like, and the way he saw it now his competitive spirit was undermining his life, and yet he seemed unable to switch it off.

Aware the phone had rung twice, he rinsed his mouth and hopped two steps before throwing himself across the bed, grabbing the mobile phone on its fourth ring. 'Hello?' At this time of night he expected it to be Drew or one of the sales team, and was confused by a strange man's voice. He thought the man might have got the wrong number, but then he was told to wait while he was put through to Gemini.

In that instant he knew he wanted to backtrack, to go back half a minute to the moments before the phone rang. He held his breath, and in the gasp that she took before she was able to utter a word he knew it had something to do with Orion, his small man. 'He's going to be all right, isn't he?'

Then he heard what he already knew. 'No,' she said.

'He's not...' He couldn't bring himself to say the word. 'He's not,' he gasped, 'is he?'

'Yes,' she said in the lightest whisper. Then he heard the phone being dropped, the sound of footsteps and nothing else that made any sense.

Clint yelled into the phone for someone to pick it up and speak to him, but no one heard. He hung up then called home again but the number was engaged. He tried again and again, impatiently hitting redial but each time the line was engaged. In a foggy haze now, his body overtaken with an uncontrollable trembling, he rang reception for Katrina's number. When they refused to give it to him he got off the bed and went down to demand it from them in person.

From a seat in the hotel lobby Clint watched the night porter phone Katrina. The lobby seemed overly bright, and Clint felt as if he were hovering under the lights of an operating theatre, anethetised but fully conscious, with no way of telling anyone how much it hurt. In what seemed like the same eternal moment the elevator beeped and Katrina glided like a ghost towards him.

She leant over and held him against her for as long as he needed, and when they pulled themselves apart Clint glimpsed tears running down her face. She led him to his room where they packed his belongings and when his phone rang she told him to answer it, then wait there for her while she collected a few things.

In the back seat of the cab on the way to the airport, Clint tried to tell her what had happened. 'I think she dropped him, but I can't be sure...'

For a while they both said nothing - the silence, like a vacuum, giving everything an absence of meaning. Katrina struggled to think of something to say; thousands of empty words running through her mind, failing to soften the shock of what couldn't be made better.

Katrina reached over and held his hand, the commonality of human experience was the only thing she had to offer. 'I know I can never know how bad this must be for you, but time will -' she wanted to say Heal but changed her mind, ' - dull the pain.' Time on its own heals nothing; grief requires more work than that.

Clint threw his head back against the headrest, both hands covering his eyes as he let out a shuddering cry. 'Please God,' he whimpered.

She swallowed hard. *Bargaining with God, she knew how often she'd resorted to that.*

Several miles went by and only the crackle of the driver's radio and Clint's raspy long sighs filled the space between thoughts. There'd be blame, denial, accusations, revenge, hatred and guilt - yet at the end of it all nothing could ever bring their baby back.

The cab pulled up outside the airport just five minutes before the boarding gates were due to close. Katrina threw some money at the driver and helped rush Clint towards the check-in counter.

Giving one quick hug, she guided him towards the departure doors, saying, without quite knowing why, 'There are several stages to grief, make sure you look after Gemini.'

Katrina waited until Clint was out of sight then walked back through the terminal, looking for a coffee shop. She sat by the window, watching a plane land on the runway; the tarmac sucking the speed from its tires as it slowed to a crawl. Then she noticed, as she had many times before, how it was impossible not to watch and at the same time feel the rapid decrease in velocity. She watched Clint's plane turn stiffly at the end of the runway. Her heart ached for him. Through the double-glazing she anticipated the noise of the engines, and felt with conflicting inevitability the powerful thrust as it graciously lifted into flight seconds later. She let out a long sigh, accepting they were all participants in a screenplay they hadn't written, in a script no one could stop.

Finishing her coffee, she wandered into the corridor just as a batch of new arrivals started filing through. The people seemed fleshier, softer, more vulnerable than usual, and in their passing she smelt a mixture of perfumes, leather, hair gel and oranges.

On her way out of the building she stopped momentarily to admire the flowers that were placed in buckets on the street. The flowers seemed more purple-hued, scarlet, orange and yellow than they ever had before. She struggled to decide on a bunch but couldn't. They were all pretty; to try to choose a single bunch made her feel too confused. Anyway they'd drip water and wilt in the sun;

she had no need for them.

Later, at the hotel, she regretted not buying the orange bunch - it was their beauty, perfection and transience that made them a celebration of life. From now on, she would make sure she had flowers, lots more flowers, in her life.

- 31 -

Clint dropped his bag to the floor. A wreath of flowers lay against one wall and he tried to figure out who would've known long enough to have arranged delivery, then told himself off. How could he wonder *that* at a time like this?

Despite all the events that'd occurred in his absence, the room seemed undisturbed. He called out and when there was no reply headed towards the bedroom. Passing the nursery door, hearing a noise, he pushed it open and then gasped, not expecting to see a large shape in the middle of the room. 'SSShh,' said Pamela, stroking Flame's brow in a hypnotic pattern. Clint watched as Flame's eyes drooped sleepily then he backed out the room and went to the kitchen and waited for Pamela to join him.

Over coffee Pamela told him all she knew and that the doctor had given Gemini a sleeping pill, she was in the bedroom. Clint finished his drink and went to lie beside her, the movement on the mattress waking her. Gemini put her arms out towards him and they held each other tightly, feeling each other's sorrow in the short clutches of breath and sighs that neither could control.

Gemini finally broke the silence. 'Sorry,' she said, the word coming out in a whisper that lingered and resonated an eternity between them.

Eventually Clint gave his reply, his voice seeming to quiver and echo far away. 'It wasn't your fault.'

For the longest time they clung together, their bodies shaking in discordant sobs until the pills took effect once more and Gemini dozed off in his arms. Later that morning they were woken by a gentle knock on the door. Pamela told them the funeral director was waiting in the lounge.

Clint guessed Mr Eaves was in his early fifties, a short thin man, he shook Clint's hand, then Gemini's, expressing his condolences. They all sat down. Mr Eaves opened his briefcase and pulled out a clipboard, telling them he had some mandatory details they'd have to complete. Gemini sat ashen white, nearly comatose, so Clint responded to the questions: full names of the father and mother, full name of the deceased, date of birth, place of birth, cause of death.

Clint's heart withered as Mr. Eaves repeated the question, 'Cause of death?' He felt as though he was being told, for the first time again, that his baby boy was dead.

Gemini opened her mouth and tried to speak but only a croaked syllable came out. She coughed, cleared her throat and tried again. 'Accidental,' she said. 'He fell from a table. It was an internal hemorrhage, he was a hemophiliac, you know.'

Mr Eaves finished writing up his notes then passed the form to Clint and Gemini to sign before putting it in his briefcase and pulling out a burgundy, leather-covered folder. Flipping the first page open, he asked if they would prefer the casket in teak or mahogany, or perhaps the children's special?

Clint looked at the small caskets, fanned in an arc on the page like a hand of cards, and he couldn't help noticing the photographer had used a special filter to create a starburst of light glinting off the tip of a gold handle.

He saw Gemini flinch when Mr. Eaves made his suggestion: 'The pretty blue one with teddy bears on it, perhaps?'

'Clint?' she asked desperately.

'Who cares about the fucking casket?' Clint yelled. 'I just want my son back...' His voice cracked and he broke down in sobs, hiding his head in his hands, frustrated there was nothing he could do to spare any of them the pain.

Mr Eaves excused himself and Gemini moved beside Clint, cradling him in her arms until he was calm.

After a while they reconvened and this time Pamela joined them and she made the decision for them; the casket would be plain white.

***

There was a knock on the door and Katrina looked up from her computer screen to see Sarah bring the mail in. Dropping a pile of letters on the desk, Sarah passed Katrina a small cream envelope decorated with pink flowers.

'You look like you need cheering up,' Sarah said, 'I suggest you read this one first.'

Katrina pulled out a photograph and a handwritten note with a flower-fairy sitting on a pink clover in the bottom right hand corner.

Dear Dr Dudek,

A year ago I had a miscarriage after an amniocentesis. Later I got the results to say that baby was normal. I felt so depressed and guilty and vowed I would never go through that again...But now Invivotest is available you have given us hope.

The problem is Fragile X runs in my husband's family and he already has one Fragile X child to his first wife. Though we love Jason dearly and share his care, we know we couldn't look after another mentally retarded child, nor could we afford it.

I am now thirty-eight years old and may not get too many chances at pregnancy but I would still like a child of my own - which is why I'm writing to say thank you for making testing risk-free, and for providing a test we can afford.

Thank you.

Amy Taylor

Katrina picked up the photograph and stared at the faces of a man and boy wearing matching purple jackets, waving happily from a yellow and red fairground car. Turning the picture over she read the caption on the back: My husband with Jason on his fifth birthday.

Rising from her chair, Katrina took the snapshot and pinned it to a corkboard on the wall, her eyes brimming with tears.

***

Gemini and Clint walked slowly to the front of the chapel with Flame snuggled quietly in Gemini's arms. Sun shone through the stained-glass windows of Jesus holding a lamb, the green-glass meadows filtering colored light across the small white casket.

Gemini coughed when the priest welcomed the congregation to the ceremony that was to 'acknowledge and celebrate the life of Orion'. Fighting back the rising bile, she refused to believe this could be called a celebration.

The priest read some prayers and readings then Clint said a few words, pausing to wait for two latecomers to maneuver themselves between the narrow pews. Gemini turned to give them the same glassy smile she'd given everyone that day. Only after a short delay did she realise one of the men was Hudson; his presence making her mind feel even more distant from her body as she registered the fact she felt no kinship with her own twin brother. She closed her eyes and took several deep breaths, willing herself to be strong, if only for Flame's sake.

Clint sat down and other friends of the family stepped forward to offer their tributes. Katrina said a few words then Adam took the microphone from her.

'As a hemophiliac, I have lived all my life knowing it could be a short one. For years I struggled with the unfairness of it until I realised that fighting reality was a waste of time. All I know with clarity is I might as well enjoy every ounce of life God has given me right here, right now. The Chinese have a saying: Don't try to steer the river. To not accept Orion's passing is to not accept the flow of life.'

'In the end I think what is most important is that we offer Gemini, Clint and Flame the emotional and spiritual support they need to accept this truth and to carry on with life in the true spirit it is intended.'

Adam sat down, and the priest wound up the ceremony with a short prayer and invited the congregation to join the family at the reception. To the sounds of 'The Teddy Bear's Picnic' Gemini and Clint approached the small casket, giving it one last stroke before walking up the aisle to stand at the entranceway.

Slowly the rest of the congregation filtered to the front; some left flowers, toys, poems, drawings or photographs beside where Orion lay.

The reception was held in a cottage at the back of the chapel. On a table at the front of the room there was a selection of food and drinks, and classical music played in the background as the guests took turn hugging and consoling Gemini and Clint. Flame was pinching Clint's nose and acting grumpy and bored when Katrina went over.

'You need a break, let me take her to the playground out the back,' Katrina said, holding her hands out to take the baby from him. Clint hesitated. 'Promise I won't bite,' Katrina said. Clint smiled, then led Katrina to the buggy. Putting Flame in he showed Katrina how to buckle the safety harness before heading outside. For a while Katrina battled with the wheels on the broken paving stones before hitting her stride, inwardly cursing how ridiculous she must look, fully dressed in a suit.

Approaching the play area, a couple of young boys noisily ran up the steel steps of a slide before throwing themselves down the chute and running back up for another turn.

'Mommy, look at me!' yelled the first boy.

'Mommy, look at me!' mirrored the younger one, a stubby-legged boy in baggy shorts.

A fair-haired woman in her late twenties looked in their direction and smiled while continuing to push a toddler in one of the baby swings.

Pulling up alongside, Katrina took Flame and placed her into the spare swing. After the first push Flame flopped forwards, her chin resting on the harness in front, her back still not strong enough to hold her head up for long periods of time. Katrina adjusted Flame's position and held her there as she very gently swayed the swing back and forth. Flame let out a happy squeal at this newfound sensation and Katrina's heart lifted as she shared the baby's uncomplicated moment of delight.

'Higher, higher,' screeched the little boy on the other swing. The fair-haired lady smiled at Katrina and said, 'It never ends, does it?'

Katrina shook her head. The question didn't need a reply; the repetitive movement of the swings seemed to be an answer in itself.

'Is she your only child?' the woman asked.

On any other day that question would have been as natural as a comment about the weather, if it weren't for the fact that only moments earlier Katrina had had the thought that she was, in a metaphysical sense, somehow connected to Flame.

'I'm just minding her for a short time,' Katrina replied, tears welling in her eyes. Turning so the woman couldn't see, she unintentionally gave the swing a hard push and Flame let out a nervous cry. Katrina caught the swing and slowed its motion.

'Mom, Jason's climbing up the slide,' whined one of the boys.

'Stop that,' the young woman shouted, then blew her smaller baby some kisses.

'Isn't it a pity they don't stay this age for ever?' she said to Katrina.

Out of politeness Katrina returned her smile yet inside she rebeled at the thought of Orion's tiny casket - how wrong this woman was, and how unfair it was that anyone could have any complaints about life at all. Before she had any conscious knowledge of her mouth opening she heard herself saying: 'This little girl had a twin brother until three days ago, I've just been to his funeral. He'll always stay the same age, so just think how lucky you are.'

Realising the words she'd heard were hers, she looked away, embarrassed and confused. She stopped the swing and took Flame out and returned her to the buggy. As she fiddled with the safety harness, she noticed Flame's round cheeks, curly lips and sparkling almond eyes and felt consumed by the urge to kiss her. Under her lips Katrina felt the softness of the baby's plump pink skin and then an irrepressible sense of awe. Fighting back tears, she moved

Flame's hand to buckle the harness, noticing the dimples on her podgy knuckles, the tiny pearly nails, the perfect mechanics of that small hand - and for the first time she saw the glory of childhood and all its possibilities for laughter, intimacy and wonder.

Ignoring the woman's stares, Katrina turned abruptly and stumbled back along the path. Walking slowly, giving herself time to regain her composure, she allowed herself the thought that she'd never pushed a baby buggy before, never wanted to either - not until now, she thought. Somewhere along the way she'd excluded the possibility of children, yet she could think of no good reason; none other than that she'd experienced so much sadness and guilt she could never have granted herself permission to give life.

Katrina took Flame into the room and saw Gemini talking to a woman wearing a hat. Drawing closer Flame recognised her mother and started to wriggle. Gemini broke her conversation and put her hands out to receive her baby, as she did so the person under the wide-brimmed hat turned towards Katrina.

'Mom, I'd like you to meet Katrina. Katrina, this is my mother, Pamela.'

Katrina caught her breath. Even under the hat, the arched eyebrows, and prominent nose - enlarged and reddened from grief - were unmistakable. They shook hands and Katrina searched the other woman's tear-stained face for any signs of recognition, and when she saw there were none felt her internal tension ease, just a fraction.

Later that evening Gemini knocked softly on her mother's door before pushing it open. The bedroom light was on and Pamela lay in bed, her eyes closed. 'Are you asleep?' Gemini whispered.

Blinking, Pamela stirred, then sat up. 'No, come in, honey.'

'I brought you a drink and a sleeping pill. I think you should take it,' said Gemini. 'I'm going to take one. I think we need all the help we can get to keep our sanity over the next few weeks. For Flame's sake…'

'Hopefully she's too young to realise…' Pamela stopped. Perhaps she'd heard it too - the word 'hopefully' hanging in the air, out of context, and out of place, just like all the other platitudes that'd been said over the last few days.

Pamela's hand trembled as she raised the cup to her mouth. Gemini squeezed her eyes tight to hold in another round of tears. Suddenly tired of all the crying and sadness that surrounded her, she changed the subject, talking about some of the people who'd been at the reception - especially Adam, whom Pamela had talked to at length. After a while Pamela yawned, and Gemini guessed the pill was starting to take effect so she kissed her mother goodnight.

Gemini was leaving the room when Pamela asked drowsily, 'Oh, Gem - that woman, Katrina, have I met her before?'

'I don't think so, she's Clint's boss,' Gemini replied. Then she had the thought that her mother could have seen her on television, so she suggested that.

'Perhaps that's why she seemed familiar,' Pamela replied in a voice that sounded close to sleep.

Gemini switched off the light and closed the door quietly behind her.

- 32 -

Throughout Orion's funeral Katrina had tried to fathom her feelings but could not. Her mind, racing out of control, trying to match words to thoughts until finally she surrendered to the notion that death - like life - had no meaning that could be measured and quantified. Life is not a commodity; its existence is more that.

Now, sitting side by side in a wine bar booth, Scott lifted his arm away to give Katrina room to move to search for a tissue in her handbag. She knew the truth was she'd been crying for herself - and her sadness at the thought she might die an empty shell, unloving and unloved.

'I used to think that if we knew from the beginning that a life was to be cut short there was no point to it. But sitting in the chapel today made me realise how much meaning there is in the first breath, first step, first tooth,' Katrina said. 'Today I saw myself in a new light - and I was ashamed. Ashamed of the way I pity and judge people when I have no right. I've always thought I've known what's best for everyone else when it's up to them to decide,' she said, before breaking down into soulful tears, resting her head on Scott's broad shoulder.

When Katrina looked up she saw he'd been crying too and she wondered what his tears were for - can sadness be transmitted by osmosis? Was grief better shared?

Smudging the last tear from her cheek with a corner of a sodden tissue Katrina knew she had to act on the revelation she'd had that day. She picked up her glass and gulped her drink down in three large swallows before taking Scott's hand in hers. Holding his gaze, she drew the strength to tell him what she'd never dared tell him before - that she loved him; she wished she knew a way to show him, but even if he didn't love her back she would love him anyway.

Each day as Gemini threw out dying flowers she felt lonelier and lonelier. The phone rang less and fewer people called around. There were uncomfortable moments in even the simplest routines: buying milk and bread from the local shop, going to the hairdresser's, filling the car with gas. Even Luigi at the pizza parlor didn't know how to respond to her. When she tried to pay he just waved her on. 'Gratios,' he said, kindly.

Flame appeared happy. Smiling and chuckling she'd throw her toys from the highchair as she used to, seeming to have no inkling Orion wasn't there. At times Gemini thought her behavior was better than before, but perhaps that was an illusion with only half the work to do now.

For something to do one day Gemini called into her old place of work and had lunch with two of the women who filled her in on all the gossip. Both said they were sad about Orion, and while they cooed over Flame even more went unsaid.

Of all their friends and relatives, Adam was the most helpful. He would phone or call around regularly with books on death and dying, and would often just sit at the kitchen table drinking coffee, saying very little, simply stroking Gemini's hand, offering sympathy.

She appreciated his concern, always affirming her grief rather than trying to deny it. His life experiences of hemophilia had given him a wisdom and empathy she found no where else - although sometimes she would be so consumed with sadness and anger, mourning the unfairness of Orion's genetic legacy, she'd forget Adam's similar situation. Embarrassed by her tactlessness, Adam would gently laugh and dismiss her apologies, increasing her admiration for his acceptance of his mortality. More and more she found herself drawing inspiration, and the strength to carry on living, from him.

***

Ten days after Orion's funeral Gemini opened the curtains to a beautiful summer's day. The beach was filling with mothers and children clutching their buckets and spades, towels and other paraphernalia. Even at a distance she could feel the excitement of the children dipping their toes in the water before running backwards squealing, as the cold waves rolled in to catch their feet.

Turning to look at Clint she said, 'I hate nice days, it's like I have to pretend I'm *having* a nice day.'

'But you've got to fake it, Gem. Otherwise we'd all get depressed.'

'But I'm not depressed, I'm sad. There's a difference. Why can't I just be sad?'

'Because you being sad makes us sad too. It reminds us *why* - and deep down we're all shit-scared of the thing that made you sad. So we pretend we're happy and that none of the rest of us is going to die.'

'Well, here's to another fan-bloody-tastic day in paradise,' she said, flicking the quilt to make the bed. She could hear Flame begin the first of what they called her 'start-up' cries that would allow them two minute's grace before the unedited version. 'Listen to that,' said Gemini.

'What?' asked Clint.

'Her crying.'

'What's wrong with it?'

'There's only one. I don't think I'll ever get used to just one cry, one bottle, one kid to bath and dress. I feel so incomplete, and if that's how I feel how do you think Flame feels?'

Clint stood with his back to her, staring blankly into the closet. She guessed he must have forgotten what he'd gone to the closet for and felt a clutch in her stomach; he looked so vulnerable. 'Clint?'

'What?'

'Oh, nothing. I just thought you'd gone to sleep on the job,' she said.

He turned and stepped towards her before he collapsed onto the bed, all pretense of happiness gone. Gemini put her arms round his slouched and sorrowful body and comforted him like a baby.

'Clint, tell me, what's the matter?'.

'I don't know, Gem. I feel so…guilty. If I hadn't taken this stupid job I would've been there to help you…and you…might not have…dropped him like that. I can't forgive myself, Gem…I can't…'

Gemini stroked his neck, rocked him, making soothing noises to reassure him. The same thoughts had haunted her but she knew they served no purpose, there was no one to blame.

On Saturday night Minstrel was so happy to see Katrina he jumped up, leaving a gray smudge on the front of her white skirt. Scott apologised even though she wasn't at all bothered about the stain; she liked the way Minstrel treated her as part of the family.

When they were inside Katrina was flattered by the trouble Scott had gone to tidying the room and setting the table with candlesticks, flowers, and his best china and cutlery. She enjoyed the simple meal he'd prepared: pasta with salad, and raspberries and ice-cream for dessert. After they'd finished eating Scott took her through to his lounge and they sat on cushions, drinking red wine. This time she noticed an intimacy in the way he looked and listened to her, and later that night Katrina's heart jumped when he touched and kissed her with the passion of a man, and a lover.

Just after midnight, not daring to make any assumptions, Katrina prepared to leave. With her car keys in one hand, she started walking to the door.

'Stop where you are,' Scott said. 'Close your eyes, I have something I want to give you.'

Waiting in the middle of the room, Katrina heard him open and close a drawer then she felt the warmth of his breath on her face as he placed a light, cold object in her hands.

'You're not allowed to open your eyes until you know what it is,' he said.

Katrina ran her fingers round the small metallic object; it had a round center, with several spikey pieces attached, like the petals of a flower.

'The love-me, love-me-not clock,' she said, huskily, 'I thought you must've forgotten....' Her words withered away as Scott pulled her close to him, kissing her fully, showing his desire. And as he led her to the bedroom, her spirit flew with an exhilaration that came from a closeness she'd never felt from him before.

- 33 -

Katrina held the phone up to her ear, her other hand pushed the paperweight across her desk; she'd used it to crush a small piece of biscuit and was now taking aim to drop the crumbs off the edge. As she waited for Steen to answer his phone she turned the paperweight over to blow the last traces of crumbs from its underside before setting it back in its rightful place on her desk.

'Hello?' queried Steen, sounding as if he only half-expected the caller to have waited so long.

'Steen.'

'Katrina?' By the question in his tone she guessed he wasn't expecting her call. 'What's happening?'

'That's what I want to know.'

'What do you mean?'

'Our stocks have dropped forty-percent in the last few hours. Didn't you know?'

'Oh, that,' he said, sounding annoyed.

'Do you know why?' she asked.

'No,' he said. 'You tell me.'

'Well there's nothing out of the ordinary happening this end. I thought you must know something I don't.'

'Why should I?' he asked in such a way that she thought he was mocking her. 'Prices drop like this all the time, there doesn't have to be a reason for it.'

Giving him the benefit of the doubt she tried a new approach. 'This might sound silly to you, but it's just that I get the feeling we've been dumped.'

'Dumped?' he said, in a tone that made him sound as though he'd never considered the idea, the next moment making it perfectly clear he knew exactly what she meant. 'Well, yes, you could put it that way. You've been dumped.'

'But why?'

'I don't know, they're investors, Kat,' he said, 'they can do what they like with their money.'

'Opportunists, more like,' she said.

'Possibly.'

'Sharks.'

'No,' he said sternly, 'this is business. They're profit-takers moving on to the next best thing.'

She kept quiet.

'There's nothing personal in this. Come now, Katrina, you of all people should know that. Ego has nothing to do with prices on the stock market; you've just got to look at the fundamentals.'

'Our fundamentals are fine.'

'That might be how you and I see it, but that's not necessarily the way the punter sees it - some of them can't see longer than the end of the day. Some even less than that.' He stopped for a moment, but she didn't trust herself to reply to that superior tone of voice. 'Katrina,' he said, soothingly, dripping condescension, 'it's just a normal day, there's nothing unusual in a small drop.'

The hairs on the back of her neck tingled. She knew that type of calm - fake - and even though she was several miles away she could see the smile on his face.

'You mean they're only giving us three months to prove ourselves? We haven't even started the consumer campaign. Surely after one slow quarter they don't think we're history?'

When he didn't reply, she asked him again, 'Steen?'

'What?'

'Do you mean to tell me that after one slow quarter they think we're history?'

'You're an intelligent woman - you figure it out.'

'Stop kidding me Steen. With all those computer programs and Wall Street analysts on your team, you know this isn't some blip out of the blue. What's going on?'

Still he refused to answer and she wondered how he could act so cool when he must be losing money too. 'Steen?' She heard him breathe heavily as though he was going to explain. Then when he didn't respond she lost her patience, snarling, 'Someone's going to get rich out of this, for God's sake, we've gone lower than the list price and for no good reason. I want to know who's doing this to us, and why.' Still there was no reply, but this time the silence sounded absolute and she knew that no amount of cajoling over the phone would work.

Flame had cried most of the night from teething pains; unable to get much sleep, Clint had started work this morning at six. Now, after a four-hour session of sales forecasts, he felt as if he'd been there all day yet it was only ten o'clock.

Checking his e-mail he saw an alert that told him INUT stocks had dropped to a new low, they were now less than the list price.

Katrina came into his office appearing distressed. 'You've got to look at these,' she said, handing him a couple of letters.

Clint immediately recognised the letterhead. 'It's from the medical journals,' he said, trying to steady his eyes long enough to concentrate on the printed words.

Katrina didn't respond. At any other time she'd have chided him for uttering such a pointless statement.

Scanning the letters, he gathered the publications would no longer accept their advertising; they'd received a petition from 4,500 physicians who threatened to boycott readership of the journals if they continued to publish the Invivotest advertisements.

'Got any bright ideas?' she asked.

He shrugged. 'We can't fight them in the newspapers; that'd make our stockholders nervous. We'll have to be more discreet - increase the direct mail and make sure Drew lets the sales team know what's going on.' He paused for a while to think, then added,

'We'll have to rely on the public for their support when we run the consumer campaign.'

Katrina looked pale so he pointed to an empty chair. 'What's wrong?' Her eyes watered and she sniffed loudly. Clint moved a pile of papers, found some tissues hidden underneath and tossed the box the last few inches to land within her reach. 'Here, catch!'

Katrina tugged a tissue free and blew her nose. She seemed uncoordinated, and while Clint wanted to do something to make it easy for her, easy for him, he didn't know what.

'Perhaps we should give up now, save ourselves the grief of going against the tide,' she said, despondency thickening her voice.

Clint sighed. He wanted to reassure her, tell her she was just having a bad day but he couldn't cheat the truth. Instead he said nothing.

Katrina said quietly, 'I remember a study a few years ago where the researchers asked cystic fibrosis sufferers if there was a test to identify whether their offspring would inherit cystic fibrosis, would they take the test. Eighty percent said they would. But when the test became available only twenty percent did.' She paused to use another tissue. 'Why do people want to bury their heads in the sand? Why, when we're giving them the chance to save themselves so much pain in their lives, why is there so much opposition to that idea?'

Clint looked at her helplessly then made a philosophical comment about no one having all the answers. After a while Katrina got up and left and Clint sat staring at a desktop photograph of Gemini and Flame. Suddenly he hated the picture. He hated it for its newness and the way it reminded him of the older snap it replaced; both twins as newborns cradled in Gemini's arms. A lump formed in his throat and a wave of self-pity washed over him. He regretted it now, all that time he'd missed.

The phone rang and he let it ring five times before picking it up. But when he tried to say his name he found he couldn't speak. He quickly replaced the phone, tried to mentally compose himself, knowing whoever was on the other end would think the operator had cut them off.

When the phone rang again, he was ready.

The call was from the president of the United Pharmacy Wholesalers Guild. They'd received a petition from physicians who would boycott members who didn't remove Invivotest from their shelves. He wanted to know, on behalf of their members, the procedure for stock returns. Clint noticed he wasn't asked if he would accept the returns, he was simply asked how. And how could he refuse? Listening carefully he tried to think of a way to get them to reverse their decision, because if they refused to stock the test, how many others might do the same?

'As a professional group, don't you have some ethical problems about being bullied?' He tried to sound as if he was concerned for them, their loss of autonomy.

Clint heard a cynical laugh on the other end of the phone. 'Do you think we actually have a choice?'

He was right, Clint knew that, and no amount of wishing otherwise would change that fact. Desperately he tried another approach. 'So how does your group feel about such standover tactics? Doesn't it set a precedent for the future?'

The line went quiet. Clint had no way of knowing if he'd struck a chord or caused offense. He held his breath and waited for what seemed like minutes. In the end he was forced to ask: 'Are you still there?'

'Yes, I'm still here.' There was another long pause during which Clint decided not to pursue the subject, and in the next exchange he agreed to accept delivery of the returns.

In his mind he could see tomorrow's headlines:
PHYSICIANS BOYCOTT ABORTION TESTS
DRUG STORES BAN FETAL TESTS
INUT GETS ITS COME-UPPANCE

- 34 -

'How could you?' yelled Gemini, tossing the newspaper across the table. Clint looked up to see the paper sliding at speed towards him. He tried to grab it but a corner veered into his orange juice, knocking it over. The glass smashed onto the table, the tinkling noise adding dramatic effect.

Gemini turned to pick up a cloth then let out an angry grunt as she threw it at him as hard as she could before storming out of the room. Clint dabbed at the paper and then dropped the cloth over the top of the spill. At first he couldn't see what she was referring to, then his eye caught a headline at the bottom of the page.

DIRECTOR SEEKS SYMPATHY VOTE WITH SON'S DEATH. *Physicians and pharmacists throughout the country are threatening to boycott readership of two national medical journals that have accepted advertising for a new fetal diagnostic test, Invivotest. Physicians have also withdrawn support from pharmacies prepared to stock and sell the test direct to the consumer.*

A spokesperson for the National Medical Association, Dr Willcott says that while Invivotest is a useful medical test the Association is opposed to the marketing of the product which will allow patients to receive the full genetic details of their fetus without the supervision of a registered medical practitioner.

United Pharmacy Wholesalers Guild say they support the physician boycott and members of the guild will be removing Invivotest from their shelves today.

Inuterogene, the manufacturers of the prenatal test, refused to comment on the boycott although the marketing director, Mr Clint Harrison, said he believed all parents would benefit from the fetal DNA test. Mr Harrison and his wife gave birth to twins earlier this year. One of the twins was diagnosed with hemophilia at birth and the boy died just weeks ago. 'With DNA testing many parents could be spared the pain I experienced,' he said. For the complete story turn to section B1.

Clint turned to section B1 and scanned the contents - there was an extended interview with Dr Willcott, a picture of a woman pricking her finger with Invivotest, a drawing of a fetus and an overview of historical landmarks in genome testing. Apart from the front-page headline there was nothing Clint hadn't expected - in fact he even felt slightly relieved.

He took the paper with him to find Gemini. She was lying face down on the bed.

'What can I say, Gem? I did warn you,' he said, knowing that though she wouldn't reply she was listening to every word, utterance and intonation. 'You know how the press sensationalises everything, this'll blow over soon enough, we should try and keep things in perspective... '

'Keep things in perspective?' Gemini hissed, pushing herself up to face him, pure fury flashing in her eyes. 'You exploit your son's death for commercial gain and you call that keeping things in perspective?'

That wasn't what he'd meant. 'But they distorted what I said, you know I never meant any harm.'

She ignored his feeble excuses. 'Are you saying you wish Orion had never been born? What's Flame supposed to think when she's old enough to read and realises her own father would've selectively aborted her brother if he'd known? Or would you have eliminated them both?'

She glared at him and he knew that whatever he said right now would never be right, could never be. A burning sense of frustration raged through him and he felt the urge to strike something. Instead he clenched and unclenched his fists. 'You know that's not what I feel, you're making too much out of it.'

'Am I?' Gemini shrieked, her voice waking Flame who'd been napping in the nursery. 'I wouldn't have missed a minute of Orion's life, and I'd live it all over again if only I could.' Gemini got off the bed abruptly. 'I've had enough - I can't believe I married such a heartless bastard,' she said, striding out the room.

Clint heard a door open and a few seconds later her voice calming Flame. With a sigh he went back to the kitchen. Out the corner of his eye he saw Gemini take Flame into their bedroom and he heard things being moved around in angry bursts. He'd only just tidied the table when Gemini came through with a bag slung over one shoulder and Flame on the other.

'Are you leaving?' he asked, tired of the struggle.

She gave him a defiant glare that turned to a look of disdain when she realised that with both hands full she needed him to open the door.

He opened it. 'When are you coming back?'

'When I feel like it,' she said haughtily. He shrugged. To care any more right now would take more energy than he had.

Steen had already been shown to a table when Katrina arrived at the restaurant, fifteen minutes late. He sat with his back to a wall-panel aquarium of tropical fish that swam among globes that glittered, emulating the night sky.

He stood to greet her, giving her a glancing kiss on one cheek which she returned, feigning delight at seeing him.

'It's so surreal,' she said, sitting down, looking beyond him at the fish, genuinely enchanted by the soothing sound of the water filters and the soft lighting the aquarium cast within the room.

Steen turned to look behind him. He seemed tense. 'Oh, the fish!' he said. 'I wondered what you meant for a moment then.'

'You've seen the papers then?' she asked.

He nodded in his usual cool manner, his eyes told her nothing.

'What are you going to do about a distribution channel?' he asked.

'We'll sell direct.'

'From the warehouse?'

She shrugged. 'Why not?'

'You'll need more funds,' he said, and their eyes met for the longest time.

'Yes,' she said eventually, still holding his gaze.

'Is that what this lunch is all about?'

'Yes.' There was no need to apologise. It was, after all, the simple truth.

'The problem is, Katrina, we're already way too exposed in biotech. The risk-return ratios are too high right now. As a company we need a more balanced portfolio, we simply can't afford to put more money into your sort of venture - it would jeopardise our own financial stability.' He paused, and as Katrina looked past him she saw an angelfish swim towards her. It opened its pink lips into a circle and kissed the glass before turning sharply, receding into a darkened globe.

'You've changed your tune,' she said.

'Not really,' he said looking uncomfortable.

'When I phoned you yesterday about the drop in share price that was the start of all this, wasn't it?'

He gave a noncommittal shake of the head.

'I think you know something I don't, what is it Steen. Please…'

He fidgeted with his placemat.

'You can't lie to me, we're friends. Please tell me.'

'Nothing,' he said. 'There's nothing.' He stood to go to the bathroom, another sure sign of nervousness she thought. But when he returned and resumed their conversation she noticed he had a steel edge in his voice; he'd firmed his resolve. 'The thing is, Katrina, we want to pull the plug. As I said earlier the company is over-exposed.' He took his time taking a sip of water. 'And we've been approached by a company that would be interested in purchasing Inuterogene.'

'What, even now? Even after the last few days?' she asked.

He nodded. 'I had confirmation from them just an hour ago.'
'Who?'
'I'm not at liberty to say.'
'What do you mean?'
'Simply that. It's a shell company and even I don't know for sure who's behind them.'
'But they've got the money?'
He nodded again.
'It would be a very good offer,' he replied. She was aware of a waiter hovering behind her, and while she never saw a wink of the eye, a motion of the head or flick of the hand she knew Steen must've given him a signal to stay away.
'Do we have a choice?'
'You could try and raise some finance elsewhere…'
'But we'd need your approval first?'
'Essentially,' he said. *Essentially* - what a coward, he can't even say a straight yes.
'What about my staff, what would happen to them?'
'In research and development it would be business as usual. As for sales and marketing…I expect they'd be well looked after.'
'And me?'
'You'd be a very wealthy woman.'
She looked over his shoulder at a goldfish and watched as bubbles of air popped out of its mouth and ascended soundlessly to the surface. After a while she asked, 'Where did we go wrong?'
He shrugged. 'You tried.' Anger surged through her. With those two gratuitous words, he'd trivialised all her efforts.
'What does that mean?' she said sharply.
'Work it out for yourself,' he said.
Katrina watched him stab a slice of tomato onto his fork and lift it to his mouth; she felt repulsed by him. Clearly, she'd lost the chance if she'd ever had one, of getting him to share that confidence.
'You know, I trusted you,' she said. 'I thought we were friends.'
Steen slowly finished chewing his mouthful.

'When will you bring me the offer?' she said.

'I've got a few loose ends to tie up, how about Thursday afternoon? I have it on good authority the purchaser is looking for an early settlement.'

'Three o'clock,' she said. 'I'll call the members of the Board.' They both knew she'd be able to get them together at a moment's notice. Then she asked him why the rush - but though his reply included something about not wanting any press, staying out of the public arena and canceling the consumer campaign, he never properly answered the question.

'They want to let things cool down a while,' he said, coyly, making her wonder then whether he'd received confidential information, or given it.

'Funny when you think about all that advice you gave me to make sure we were protected from a hostile takeover bid,' she said, watching him carefully for a reaction, wanting to see if he would admit his guilt, his complicity.

He looked her evenly in the eyes and she learnt nothing - this was business as usual for him.

Katrina finished lunch with Steen and caught a cab straight back to work. Her mind was spinning, but beneath it there was a calm that hadn't been there before.

Breaking the news to Clint she felt unexpected relief, the opposite to how she thought she should feel.

Quite naturally Clint had asked: 'Who's the client?'

'He wasn't at liberty to say,' she said facetiously.

Clint smiled at her imitation. 'It's Zenogen, it has to be.'

She pulled a face. 'Who cares? It's not as though we've got a lot of choice.'

'Does anyone know who's backing them?' he asked.

Katrina shrugged. 'Someone bigger than us obviously.'

'An insurance company?' Clint persisted. 'The government - the military - is that why he won't say?'

'I don't know,' she said, wondering if the real issue had always been about planning and policing, genetics being the ultimate tool?

'Are we just the fall guys?' Clint asked. 'Was this his plan all along?'

'I wondered that too.'

'Why would anyone want to buy us?' asked Clint. 'The difficulties we've faced aren't going to go away.'

'No,' she said. For a few moments neither spoke, and in the silence they could hear the phones ringing and Sarah's bright spiel as she greeted each caller as if today were any other ordinary day.

'My guess is they'll wait a while, take the sting out of the market. Perhaps they'll find a way to make it compulsory,' she said, noticing how distant her voice sounded, as though she didn't really care. 'How do you feel, Clint, I mean personally?'

Clint shifted the family photo on his desk to another position before he replied. 'I wasn't planning to mention it, but Gemini and I have been having a few difficulties just lately,' he said.

'I am so sorry,' Katrina said, 'I had no idea.' But then she wouldn't have expected to have, he'd always been the consummate professional never letting his personal life interfere.

Clint forced a smile. 'You never know, perhaps redundancy would be a good thing…What about you?'

Katrina took a while to compose her answer. 'I could get upset about the fact I'm not indispensable, but the truth is I'm tired of fighting the world when really I should make peace with myself first.'

Outside the phone rang. After a while, Katrina added, 'I think I might finally have learnt my lesson: Everyone projects their own fear and pain onto life…From now on Invivotest will just have to go on without me.'

When Clint saw Gemini's car in the driveway his spirits lifted instantly. She was back and nothing else mattered.

He parked his car and rushed inside ready to grab Gemini in his arms and tell her he was a free agent, they could start afresh. But instead he stopped in his tracks as Gemini looked up at him from the sofa, wiping her nose with a tissue, her eyes red from crying.

She stood and ran to him and he took her in his arms and hugged her close, and in between shuddering sobs she told him Adam was in a critical condition in intensive care at the hospital.

Too shocked for words Clint waited for Gemini to gather the strength to tell him what had happened. Eventually she managed to control the wobble in her voice enough to tell him how she and Flame had taken Adam out to lunch and were driving Adam home when Gemini remembered she'd forgotten to buy some diapers. Unable to park close to the entrance of the store, she gave him some money to run in while she went around the block before picking him up. On her return she'd heard ambulance sirens behind her and had pulled over to let it pass, only moments later being horrified to catch a glimpse of Adam's patterned shirt as he was being lifted on a stretcher into the vehicle.

Gemini paused and Clint swallowed back his own shocked feelings of powerlessness at the thought that, in the end, fate was non-negotiable. Gemini resumed the story, telling him how she'd followed the ambulance to the hospital, later going to intensive care and learning that a car had reversed into Adam and knocked him over. The doctors were tending to him but he was unconscious with internal injuries and only next of kin were allowed in.

For the rest of the evening Clint and Gemini attempted to talk, trying to sound natural when nothing was. By comparison to whatever Adam was going through, Clint's news about Inuterogene seemed shallow and inconsequential and while Clint would've liked Gemini to tell him how she felt about him now she was back, it seemed unfair to even ask.

Before going to bed Gemini called the hospital and was told Adam's condition was still critical. She asked to speak to his mother but the telephonist was unable to transfer the call to the room she was in so the nurse promised to pass on her best wishes and give her Gemini's number.

For several hours that night Clint lay in the dark unable to sleep, thinking about Gemini's homecoming, how he wished it'd been different and that despite his concern for Adam it was hard not to feel jealous of the fondness she clearly felt for him. He knew it was uncharitable to begrudge Gemini the friendship, and he'd only just resolved to make more of an effort to get to know Adam and to appear more grateful, when the phone rang. Clint looked at the flashing digital clock: 2:46 a.m. and his throat tightened as he answered the call, no one phones with good news at that time of night.

- 35 -

Daylight sneaked through a gap in the curtains and Flame lay contentedly sucking her thumb, curled snugly under her ladybird blanket.

In the next room, Gemini cursed and shoved the dress she was holding back into the closet, before pulling out another one. First Orion, now Adam - nothing she owned seemed suitable to wear. And now, to make matters worse, Pamela had called to say she'd missed her flight and would be unable to babysit Flame while they were at the funeral.

Having no alternative, Gemini phoned Clint to tell him he'd have to miss the longest parts of the ceremony, where it was inappropriate to take Flame. He was in a meeting with Katrina when she called, but when Katrina heard of their predicament she volunteered to care for Flame, saying it was the least she could do to help.

The mourners convened at the hospital chapel; in his will Adam had appointed his hematologist and trusted friend, Dr Miles, to oversee the proceedings. His instructions included a treasure hunt complete with clues and a map, and a bus for transport. Included on the tour was a playground where the group had to play a round of hide-and-seek, Adam's favorite game as a small boy. Another clue led them to Adam's junior school where a teacher recounted many humorous tales of Adam's excuses for being late with his homework because of his late nights at the hospital. Afterwards they went to the hemophiliac meeting rooms where a woman paid tribute to Adam for the counseling he'd given her when she lost her own son. She unveiled a bronze plaque bearing the inscription: Don't try to steer the river.

Their final destination was the North Harbor lookout point where they were told it was Adam's wish that his body be cremated, his ashes scattered out at sea.

A black-edged cloud crossed the rapidly darkening skies and Gemini shivered in the rising wind. Adam's mother leant back against a coin-operated telescope, trying to find a dry spot in her handkerchief while the group waited for her.

Behind them a car pulled into the parking bay and two children ran out, banging their doors and screeching in high-pitched voices. A man's voice told them to be quiet, there were some footsteps, and then two doors slammed and the car pulled out again.

A few drops of rain fell in isolated splats onto the concrete pathway. The traffic on the road behind continued unabated, and in the relative quietness Adam's mother read them a short poem Adam had always liked. 'It's written by an anonymous author,' she said, lifting the page closer to her face, projecting her voice so she could be clearly heard.

> *'Do not stand at my grave and weep,*
> *I am not there, I do not sleep.*
>
> *I am a thousand winds that blow,*
> *I am the diamond glints on snow,*
> *I am the sunlight and ripened grain.*
> *I am the gentle Autumn rain.*
> *When you wake in the morning hush,*
> *I am the swift uplifting rush*
> *of quiet birds in circling flight.*
> *I am the soft star shine at night.*
>
> *Do not stand at my grave and cry,*
> *I am not there, I did not die.'*

For a few seconds after finishing the reading everyone stood still, and then as if by mutual agreement the circle formation dissolved and people hugged, cried, kissed and tried to smile again.

No one said much on the journey back to the chapel until the bus turned into the hospital grounds, and Dr Miles took charge again, clapping his hands, he said, 'All right, that's enough sadness. I don't know about you lot, but I could do with something to eat. After that I have one last reading - one that Adam wrote for this occasion. I know he spent many hours writing this and it was very important to him. So please, as one last favor to him, stay and listen to his final words.'

The bus stopped and Dr Miles chaperoned them into a small room filled with hundreds of yellow, pink and white balloons, and a jazz trio playing in one corner. As each guest arrived they were given a glass of sparkling wine and told to close their eyes and reach in to take a silver-wrapped present from a cane wicker basket.

Three ward nurses roamed the room refilling the wine glasses as soon as they were empty. The gaiety of the champagne bubbles soon lightened Gemini's mood and though her eyes still stung from crying, the buzz of chatter and music in the room lifted her spirits and she even caught herself swinging her body in time to the music.

In a while Dr Miles called everyone to attention. 'Ladies and gentlemen, true to Adam's word we are indeed seeing his belief that we should celebrate the joy of life. It is now my privilege to read you the speech he asked me to deliver on this occasion.'

'Friends,

I thought I should start this letter to you with the introduction 'I am sorry I can't be with you today' - like they do when they beam in the absentee Grammy Award winners. It's hard not to feel a sense of high drama, as I know my words are coming to you from 'beyond the grave' as they say. But I think you all know me well enough to know this is a sincere attempt to communicate my most heartfelt thoughts in the hopes that they may help some of you. (And yeah, all right, doc, just this once you're right: I DO have one heck of a way of getting your attention!)

Dr Miles laughed in a couple of short bursts that squeezed tears from the corners of his eyes. He brushed them away with the back of his hand and took a deep breath that came out in a pig-like snort; he let out an embarrassed laugh before he continued:

'As you all should know I'm not afraid to die - in fact I planned my funeral not as some macabre form of self-torture but more as an acceptance ritual. The wrapping of the presents and the writing of this speech were a reality check and a form of emotional growing up that helped me make peace with the inevitable prospect of my own demise.

The thing I've discovered since I've given death more thought is that the only thing that really mattered was that I told the ones I love that I love them and that my soul was at peace. So I'm telling you all now: I love you. And yes my soul does feel at peace.

And have no fear: I have no intention of boring you all with my philosophies on the meaning of life. Instead I'd like you all to bear witness to this tribute to my mother and my thanks to her for a lifetime of unconditional love and selfless devotion. Words cannot go far enough in expressing the gratitude and admiration I have for her - she gave away the largest portion of her life to raise and care for me.

She always told me: 'I will always be here for you - no matter what.' And I pinned my life on those words and her commitment to me. Thank you, Mom.

I also think of my father who deserted us. I always wanted him in my life, to be there on my birthday just like he was when I was born on Christmas Eve, 1977. I include him in my obituary not because he gave me life but because, in a significant way, he denied me it. I hope that none of you ever turns your back on your responsibility to love those you bring into the world.

And I hope you will think of me on happy occasions, which is why I've left you all a small novelty candle. I hope you will light your candles a year after my passing, and when you watch the small flickering flames, please remember me.

Thank you for taking the time to honor my life.

I will love you all always,

Adam.

Dr Miles folded the handwritten pages and stepped forward to embrace Adam's mother in a spontaneous bear hug. Clint turned to look at Gemini, and in a voice that was only slightly louder than a whisper she said, 'The same...He had the same birthday as me. I never knew that.'

Interrupted by the sounds of a baby crying, she turned to see Katrina coming towards her, doing her best to carry Flame who was wriggling, her cries intensifying at the sight of Gemini. Katrina made her way through the people and passed the baby over. 'She was fine until now, I think she's hungry but she wouldn't take the bottle from me.'

Gemini kissed Flame, making her squirm and giggle. The musicians started playing again. Soon there was a casual buzz as guests prepared to leave. Gemini sat down to give Flame her bottle and Clint was thanking Katrina when Adam's mother bustled over. 'I thought I recognised you, you haven't changed a bit!' she said.

Thinking Mrs Bryant was talking to her, Gemini looked up, only to see her gazing over her head. Katrina and Clint had stopped their conversation and were staring back at Adam's mother.

'I still remember the day you pulled that Christmas tree down.'

Gemini watched Katrina's mouth drop, undignified and surprised. Mrs Bryant tilted her head to give Gemini an appraising look and said: 'This must be your daughter, all grown up.'

Gemini felt a cold tingle down her spine. Behind her she could hear Katrina mumble, 'No, really, you must be mistaken.'

But Mrs Bryant, appearing glad of a diversionary conversation, carried on regardless. 'And your son, is he here?'

For a moment it felt as though someone had hit the pause button. Clint, Gemini and Mrs Bryant all looked at Katrina, who seemed to have stalled. Her eyes narrowed and the color drained from her face.

Mrs Bryant reached out to her. 'Are you all right?'

Katrina turned towards the door. 'There's...not enough...air in here,' she said. 'I need some fresh air.' She hurried towards the exit, fumbling in her handbag until she'd found her keys. Gemini leapt to her feet, thrusting Flame into Clint's arms she pushed through the guests, not noticing their shock at her rude behavior. With several people still obstructing her path and Katrina nearly at the door, Gemini yelled out to try and stop her. 'Wait! It's true, isn't it? How long have you known?'

Katrina broke into a run, heading towards her car.

It took a few moments for Gemini to notice everyone was staring at her. She took a couple of steps then dropped into the nearest seat, trembling, suddenly overcome by weakness.

The tires caught some loose shingle on the driveway and the red car squealed onto the highway. Katrina put her foot hard down and raged to the rapid acceleration, then reluctantly slowed as she reached the tail-end of a line of cars that filled both lanes.

She leant back in her seat and adjusted her rear-vision mirror, gasping at the sight of her own unfocused eyes, seeing in them a tinge of madness coupled with fear.

The car in front pulled away and she increased her speed. Suddenly she let out a huge scream and slammed her hands repeatedly on the steering wheel, yelling, 'Damn! Damn! Damn!'

Thoughts spun through her mind, each contradicting the other, truth and reality bouncing back against denial.

I didn't know.
Yes, you did.

No, I didn't.
Deep down you did!
Do you think I really wanted this to happen?
Perhaps. Can truth ever be denied?

Finding it hard to see the white line, she pulled over to the side of the road, turned the engine off and finally gave in to the torrent of emotions that flowed through her. Her memories were as vivid as yesterday: the sound of the Christmas tree angel, the silence when she thought she'd broken it, and the relief when it started again. She could almost feel the pain of her stitches, the entanglement of the branches, then Roseanne's giggles. Yet none of it seemed remotely funny now.

Katrina had driven aimlessly that afternoon, ending up at a picnic spot at the northern end of town. She left her car and walked to the top of the pedestrian bridge and leant on the railing, looking down. It was like she'd always known her life would lead her to this point. Yet she could not jump, something inside her told her she had a choice, and another part of her whispered she didn't; in an eternal sense, there is no escape.

The reflection of streetlights shimmered on the water below. She took a flower from her corsage and threw it over the edge. For the first few seconds the petals fluttered against the wind and then the blossom twisted and twirled randomly, until it was out of sight.

That funeral had been for *her* son and Gemini was his sister. Katrina closed her eyes against the pressure that was building in her head again, an image of Orion's small casket came to mind. She wished with all her being she could bring Orion back to life, she wished she could give Gemini her son back.

Orion had been her grandson.

Katrina searched inside for a reaction but reached an impasse, Gemini's voice haunting her still: 'how long have you known?'

Pulling back from the edge, Katrina rested her body against the gray steel railing, a continuous flow of hot tears pouring down her face as she dared to consider how one decision, made so long ago - to switch the baby boys - had affected so many. She saw how one untrue thought begets another, before layer upon layer conspires to conceal the truth; a concept she couldn't possibly have conceived or understood when she was just seventeen.

She tried to feel guilty, but couldn't because she knew she'd switched the babies for one reason only, and that was to spare her baby girl the pain and sadness she'd experienced with the loss of David. His death had destroyed her in a way she didn't want anyone else to suffer.

She smoothed away the tears with her hands. To have deserted the twins at birth was one thing, but to know that the little girl risked losing her brother - as she had done - that had been just too much guilt to bear.

Katrina took a deep breath, consoling herself with the thought that perhaps in some unconscious way Gemini's soul had known Adam was her brother. She willed her blurry eyes to focus and she started walking towards her car. There was nothing she could do to undo the past, she'd suffered long enough, she was no longer prepared to accept there was a mortgage on her soul. Getting into the car, turning the engine on, she realised only she could set herself free. All that mattered now was whatever was going to happen from now on.

Katrina climbed the steps to Scott's house, loving the way Minstrel welcomed her without prejudice as he always did. As soon as she stepped inside she could tell by the way Scott greeted her that Clint must have already phoned.

Without saying anything, Scott took her by the hand and led her to the bedroom, helping her undress before putting her to bed. He left the room then returned with a tray of orange juice and a small vase of flowers.

He sat on the end of the bed and listened as she told him of the funeral, of Mrs Bryant's discovery, Gemini's reaction, and how she'd run away. She appreciated the way he listened without judgment, and she talked and cried until she no longer felt the need to.

Then Scott went and brought Katrina the phone. 'Call her,' he said.

'What shall I say?' she said, panicking, taking the phone from his outstretched hand.

He shrugged casually. 'There are some things in life that all the thinking in the world won't fix because the answers are in here,' he said, tapping his heart before he left the room, quietly closing the door.

Later that evening when Scott crawled into bed, Katrina thanked him for his understanding and his kindness. She kissed him, and while they lay with their heads on their pillows and their faces turned towards each other she told him she loved him. Several more moments went by and then he asked her to tell him the truth about one thing.

Agreeing to his request, she held her breath in anticipation. She'd always known he'd ask one day - how could she know for sure the babies weren't his? And how might he react if she honestly answered that?

Seconds later she felt him move in the bed, opening the drawer beside him, and then she heard him rattle a box of matches. A match flared and he lit a candle that sat on the bedside table, a black trail of smoke rose in the air.

'You know I'm not very good at expressing my feelings,' he said, 'but I love you… In fact I've always loved you, and I just want you to know I have no regrets for the past.' He stopped talking for a moment and gazed at her, he'd never looked more sincere. He let out a deep sigh, and the flame of the candle wavered quickly from side to side as Katrina waited for him to continue, glimpsing a trace of a tear in his eyes.

'But what I really want to know,' he said, 'is if you'd be willing to have my baby.' Katrina gasped, then drew him to her and kissed him, marveling at the breadth of his spirit, his intuition and timing.

Katrina pushed the security buzzer and waited with trepidation. Turning nervously to look around her, she fidgeted on the spot, noticing that the flowers she held in her hand had gone floppy, that they suddenly looked too formal.

Gemini came to the door, carrying Flame on one hip. She mumbled something Katrina didn't quite hear, then lifting Flame closer to her face she said much louder, 'Look, Flame, it's your grandmother.' Her voice sounded hard and brittle and, with a ripple of shock, Katrina realised this was nothing like the beginning she'd expected. She wondered if there was a right or wrong way of doing this. It was, after all, a strange situation for anybody to be in - to be inviting someone you already knew in one sense back as your mother.

Katrina intended to pass the flowers she was carrying to Gemini, but her actions were uncoordinated and Gemini suddenly had no choice but to acknowledge the dozen red tulips that were thrust in her face.

Swapping Flame for the flowers, Gemini placed them in a vase and took them through to the lounge, putting them on the coffee table. Katrina followed carrying Flame, her high heels clopping noisily across the tiles. She settled Flame on a mat with some toys then took a seat on the sofa.

For a few moments neither woman spoke then both began to talk at the same time before stopping to invite the other to speak. In the end Gemini went first. 'It's always been a long-cherished dream of mine to find my birth m-mother' her voice faltering on the word, 'but then to find out, like that, that it's you, I still can't grasp that.'

Katrina wanted to look at Gemini but dared not, fearing she would lose control herself. Instead she looked down at Flame who'd pulled herself up and was clutching onto Gemini's knee. The baby wobbled a few seconds before falling backwards onto her bottom, then crawled forwards to pull herself up again with visible delight. She gave the scene a sense of naturalness that would otherwise have been impossible, Katrina thought.

Gemini stroked Flame's head and glanced in Katrina's direction as if she was plucking up courage to say something else. Katrina waited, knowing they would have to construct their own version of this new relationship if they were to have one. What she didn't know was what Gemini might want, but she knew her well enough to fear her honesty and her volatility.

Several minutes went by, and when it seemed Gemini was stuck Katrina nervously cleared her throat. For all the public speaking she'd done, nothing was as delicate or terrifying as what she was about to say. 'Gemini, please, I wasn't looking for you so I certainly didn't expect to find you in my life already.'

She worried it was all coming out disjointed but there was no other way for her to express the suppressed emotions and thoughts of such a long-buried secret. 'I was only seventeen and I thought I'd never see you again - ' she said before correcting herself, 'I mean either of you again. At the time I just wanted to get on with the rest of my life…'

'But how could you do that?' Gemini said, her voice a menacing hiss, anger, hurt and resentment boiling over. 'How could you be so selfish?'

A clock ticked loudly in the intense silence that followed, and Katrina forced herself to remain sitting motionless, her eyes downcast like a dog handler approaching a vicious dog. She knew she couldn't hope to understand the impact her presence was having - what dreams this girl might have had, how much could she expect her to forgive?

Eventually Katrina spoke. 'At the time I just didn't know what to do. Have you any idea what that's like - to give birth and then give your babies up?' She paused, wishing Gemini would acknowledge her, wanting her approval, desperately. 'There's so much you don't understand. I lost my own twin brother, he committed suicide when I was seventeen.'

Gemini looked up, her eyes swollen and washed of color, two small slits that made Katrina feel like she could see into infinity.

'His name was David, he had hemophilia,' Katrina said.

Gemini gasped then put her hands up to hide her face.

'He suffered all his life,' Katrina said, denying the urge to reach out and hold her, too scared to move. 'As his twin I felt his pain. And I know what you think of Invivotest - but I so desperately wanted to do something with my life to spare others the grief, to at least give them the choice.' She stopped talking, barely able to breathe. Maybe justice was being served at last; it was she who had rejected Gemini all those years ago and now she was the one who might be spurned.

Gemini sniffed a few times, stood and walked out of the room. Straining her ears to listen, Katrina heard Gemini open some cupboard doors, and in a while she returned with a box of tissues that she threw onto the coffee table in front of them.

'I know this must be hard for you to understand, but at the time I was driven to succeed at the goals I had set myself,' Katrina said. Gemini rolled her eyes and Katrina involuntarily spluttered, trying to dislodge the words that were caught in the back of her throat, knowing she must not give in to the thought that cynicism and disgust might be all Gemini would ever feel for her. 'And now I'm scared. Scared you'll hate me, that you'll tell me to go away. Just when I know what a fantastic child I gave birth to…' Her voice trailed away, overwhelmed by the enormity of her regret. She leant across the table to take a tissue. At the same time Gemini reached forward and their hands met at the box, and were withdrawn in the same instant. Gemini gave Katrina a self-conscious look and then something in the atmosphere changed between them. Standing up, Gemini took a step towards Katrina, and leaning forward, she threw her arms around her. Katrina rose to hug her and for a while they clung together, each crying into the other's hair, trying to speak but with only squeaking sounds coming out in short bursts.

Eventually they separated, and as Gemini took a step back she said, 'If only I'd known.'

Part Four

- 37 -

Eight months later, Katrina looked at the calendar on the kitchen wall and counted the days since her last period. Her breasts felt tender and now that she was certain she was pregnant, she felt delight mixed with dread.

Scott was perched on a stool at the kitchen bench reading the sports section of the newspaper. He turned a page, making some comment about a game he wanted to watch later that day, and she was glad he hadn't looked up to catch the emotion welling in her eyes. She tipped the last of the coffee into the percolator and thought how glad she was he'd never asked if Gemini could have been his. If they knew for sure, either way they'd have ended up treating her differently.

She finished making his coffee and placed it on the bench beside him, deciding she wasn't ready to tell him about the pregnancy yet. The pain they had experienced just four months ago when they received their Invivotest results still stirred sad memories because that embryo had inherited the gene mutation for hemophilia.

Respecting each other's right to form an independent decision, they didn't discuss it until later that day. At the time she'd been surprised at her own indecision - now it was her facing this dilemma there seemed to be more to consider than there had been before.

Scott had been brushing his teeth when he poked his head out of the bathroom and, with toothpaste around his mouth, said, 'I think we should try again, don't you?' Retreating back inside the bathroom, not waiting for a reply, Katrina guessed he was having some difficulty regaining his composure. Afterwards Scott told her he'd decided ensoulment happened at birth - the moment the baby drew its first unassisted breath - but then he admitted he couldn't honestly tell if he really believed that or if he'd simply moved the yardstick to suit his own situation. He'd said there was one thing he'd learnt for sure: that no one can predict how they'll feel about making this decision until it happens in their own life.

As Katrina considered these things now she felt grateful she'd had no difficulty conceiving again, but she knew that the decision would be even harder to make a second time, and what if there was a third or fourth time?

Now, as she watched Scott read the paper, she had the same thoughts, only stronger. While the Invivotest couldn't be purchased directly by the public, it could be requested from a doctor. She took a sip of coffee and decided she'd only tell him of the pregnancy once she'd received the results of the Invivotest. Scott turned the last page, closed the paper and folded it in half. Katrina smiled at him and their eyes met, and as she went to tell him they were out of coffee she told him she was pregnant instead.

'I thought so,' he said quietly. His eyes creased into a gentle smile but in them she could see a shadow, a reflection of her own fear. Then Katrina thought she heard someone say that perhaps she shouldn't do the Invivotest this time; they should be glad they could have a baby of any sort, perhaps ignorance was bliss, and life was best left to chance. Then she paused and heard the talking stop, and realised she'd just said all that. And she'd meant every word.

It was a dry windy Sunday and Katrina was in the last few weeks of her pregnancy when she went for a drive with Gemini to the North Harbor lookout. Katrina was grateful their relationship had developed into an easy friendship although there had been a few tense occasions when Gemini had asked questions that Katrina either would not or could not answer. For example, she told Gemini she hadn't known the twins' father well, and she refused to tell her his name, merely saying it would do them no good dragging up the past.

Katrina and Hudson had met only twice more. Hudson admitted he'd only met her out of curiosity, later telling Gemini he wasn't especially interested in forming a new relationship - he was too old and didn't need another mother. Katrina appreciated the amount of care and tact Gemini used when she broke this news to her, and pretended she was disappointed when secretly she was relieved.

Sometimes Katrina would meet Margaret at Gemini's place when she visited. Katrina guessed Margaret might feel concerned about her grandmother status, so when she discussed this issue with Gemini she suggested Flame call her Aunty.

'After all, I'll have a playmate for her soon enough,' Katrina had said with a smile. 'Perhaps it's best they grow up thinking they're cousins, at least until they're old enough to understand. In the meantime I'll pretend to be your sister!' Gemini agreed as they both knew that story was credible having been out shopping one day when a sales assistant mistook Katrina for Flame's mother, commenting on the likeness around the eyes.

Parking at the North Harbor lookout, Gemini briefly explained its significance before asking Katrina to wait while she went to say a quiet prayer for Adam. Katrina sat in the car and pondered the irreversible consequences of her decision to swap the boys at birth, resolving once more to keep it a secret only she would know.

On the way home Katrina felt the first contractions that were to continue on and off for another ten days before she gave birth. The pregnancy had been easier this time, not at all the way she remembered it being when she was seventeen. Looking back on herself then, she remembered how desperately unhappy she'd been, but she also recognised that the angst had served her well, giving her life impetus and direction.

Since leaving Inuterogene she'd written a medical ethics handbook and had led some workshops on the subject, and she planned to do more of this type of consulting when the baby was born. However, there were days when she missed the politics of business and the adrenalin rush it used to give her. She toyed with the idea of doing some scientific research in the future, into a reproductive genetic switch that could be disabled at birth and reactivated when required - that way every newborn would be a wanted child; to that belief she'd always remain true.

- 38 -

Scott was clumsily trying to pull a plump, limp wrist through the sleeve of a baby gown when Gemini, Clint and Flame arrived at the maternity ward carrying an enormous bunch of orange and white roses. Katrina sat up while her guests arranged chairs around the hospital bed and Scott finished fussing over Monique. Flame however refused to sit still, preferring to push the bedside trolley around the room, stopping only when she jealously spied Scott pass Monique to Gemini.

Crying loudly, Flame clung to her mother's legs and refused to be placated until she saw Gemini pass the baby back. Once she was assured of her mother's undivided attention Flame stopped making any noise, and the room went almost instantly quiet and Gemini seized the opportunity to share her own piece of good news; she was pregnant again. After only a minimal amount of protesting she had agreed to invitrofertilisation to ensure the implanted embryo would be free of the hemophilia gene mutation. She beamed happily as she told them that though she could have learnt the gender of the baby, she had chosen not to know. Then a look of concern crossed her face as she mentioned the four remaining fertilised eggs that were frozen in storage at the clinic. After five years she and Clint would have to decide their fate.

Gemini gave Clint a meaningful look and then told him that to appease her conscience she was going to have them all implanted, one each year in succession.

'We'll see about that!' said Clint, hiding his uncertain feelings for the time being.

After their visitors had left Scott waited as Katrina battled with the technicalities of getting her impatient baby's mouth latched firmly around her swollen nipple. Breastfeeding was proving to be more difficult, and painful, than she'd expected.

When the moment was right, Scott told Katrina that the birth of his daughter had been the most significant event in his life, and that he couldn't wait to get them home. For a long time neither spoke, simply admiring the magnificence of their baby girl - she was, to the best of their knowledge, perfect. While they'd decided in the early stages of the pregnancy to do the Invivotest, they didn't know the results - because they knew that if they did, they might never have had her. At their request the results sat unopened in a medical file, ready, just in case the information was needed now she was born.

At the sound of a car door slamming, the black and white scraggy dog lifted his tired body off the sofa where he'd been napping the last few hours. Slithering excitedly over the wooden floorboards Minstrel insisted on pressing his cold black nose against the newborn's cheek before allowing Scott to carry Monique over the threshold for the first time.

With the last of the home renovations completed, Scott proudly made Katrina comfortable on the sofa before going to the kitchen to make her a drink. When he returned he carried a tray with a glass of water, a vase of flowers and a gift. Katrina didn't move from her position; she didn't need to, because from where she sat the outline of the love-me, love-me-not clock was clearly evident through the red cellophane wrapping.

Later, when Scott had left the room, Katrina looked down at Monique feeling a fresh fall of tears trickle down her face. And that was when she felt her heart open to its fullest; she was finally ready to receive the love of a newborn baby - the infinity of joy.

THE END

About the Author

Jane Francis has a degree in psychology with philosophy as the supporting subject. She has also completed a short-course certificate in health economics and is an award-winning creative director for a specialist direct-marketing agency with predominantly pharmaceutical clients.

Jane lives in New Zealand and is married with four children and has had personal experience of the internal conflict associated with prenatal testing. 'From Now On' is her first novel.

Jane is currently writing her next book and would appreciate interest from a literary agent or publisher. If you can help please contact the author at http://www.jane-francis.com.

Thank you for reading this book.